"What I like about the Siberia series is its accurate representation of the facts and that Philbin gets into the heads of his characters so well. Very good indeed."

Kerry R. Trainor
Assistant District Attorney &
Bureau Chief
Police Advisory Task Force
Suffolk County, New York

"Filled with mutts, maniacs and mayhem—just like I remember!"

Blake Williams, N.Y.P.D.
Retired

"Reminds me of the good old days."

Jimmy Williams, N.Y.P.D.

"Philbin's books remind me of a week old corpse keeping company with fleas on a hot day: they're moving, pungent and buzzing with life."

Jack Sturiano, PA
Medical Examiner
Suffolk County, New York

DEATH SENTENCE

Tom Philbin

FAWCETT GOLD MEDAL • NEW YORK

For Jack Sturiano

My thanks to Jack Sturiano, PA, Suffolk County and Kerry Trainor, Deputy Chief, Suffolk County District Attorney's Office. I am also very grateful to special agents Alex D'Atri and Allan J. MacDonald of the Alcohol, Tobacco and Firearms Bureau for their invaluable help in understanding the minds of mad bombers and the perilous mechanics of making bombs.

A Fawcett Gold Medal Book
Published by Ballantine Books
Copyright © 1990 by Tom Philbin

Library of Congress Catalog Card Number: 89-91546

ISBN 0-449-14510-7

Manufactured in the United States of America

First Edition: April 1990

CHAPTER 1

In the Fresh Meadows section of Queens, one of the five boroughs that make up New York City, there are a number of interconnected fields that thus far have escaped the realtors' romantic attentions, for reasons that are anyone's guess.

But there they are, large areas of grass and trees and water, a green testament that Mother Nature can do quite nicely, even in the middle of New York City.

But the fields were not green this bitterly cold midnight in February. Everything was white and quiet from the snow that had fallen all day, and still fell lightly now from a maroon, almost black sky. In the distance, across bodies of water, there were smudged yellow house lights and lights lining highways not far from the fields, but the quintessential feeling was of quiet, quiet and loneliness. No one should be out on a night like this.

But someone was, a man on his knees in the middle of the bitterly cold quiet whiteness.

The man was motionless, and might have been mistaken for a tree stump, or a pile of garbage covered with snow.

The only things moving, ever so slightly, were his lips and his fingers, which were on rosary beads.

The man should have been a block of ice. He had been kneeling for two hours and the temperature had hovered around fifteen degrees. But he wasn't. He was oblivious to pain and discomfort. In fact, he welcomed them. It was all for the greater glory of God, and he felt an inner glow of warmth as he basked in the love and understanding of Jesus, protector and nurturer of

1

all living creatures, most especially children.

But beneath the glow was the sadness he was feeling, and he knew God was feeling, for the little creatures floating in the warm dark fluid of their mothers' wombs. Their world would be pierced, opened up to the light, and they would cry and die and crash out of the womb in Niagaras of blood and slimy tissue.

The man's eyes filled with tears, and he knew that there were tears on the face of God, as He contemplated how another baby would die, never to walk on the earth, never to live, to breathe, to think, to suckle on its mother's teat, to see a bird in a sky, an orange sunset, to know the love of its mother and father, nor ever to glory in the adoration of God. A soul that would never be, its last resting place a dumpster in the back of a sleazy building somewhere in hell.

Who knew, he thought, but that among the babies that had been murdered was the baby who would grow up to be the doctor who would have the cure for cancer or AIDS, or the one who would rush into a burning building and save a little girl, or the person who would one day grow up to be the pope, spiritual leader of the Catholic world? Or another Mother Teresa, another Einstein, another saint?

Who knew? No one would ever know, because the person who might be one of those people would have its tiny life cut off by some greedy godless bastard of a doctor, who would care for it no more than he would care if he were cleaning a turkey.

Who knew, he thought, because the godless whores —these spick sows and nigger Jabba the Hutts and white trash with bad teeth and flat asses did not care about the blessed life that bloomed and blossomed inside them. They cared for nothing except satisfying their lusts, spreading their blotched thighs, receptacles for the spurts of godless men who might just as well stick their dicks in bags of warm chicken guts.

His fingers stopped and he held a bead.

Oh ... oh ... oh ... Hail Mary full of Grace, the

2

Lord is with thee. Blessed art thou amongst women and blessed is the fruit of thy womb, Jesus. Holy Mary Mother of God, pray for us sinners now and at the hour of our death, Amen.

His fingers stopped.

But someone had to care about those little babies who would never see the light of God's day. Someone had to show love for them by stopping the cruel termination of their unborn lives.

Someone had to stop it. Someone had to send a message from God.

The man's head dropped to his chest. Tears flowed freely, hot against the cold skin. A bottomless sadness surrounded him; a bottomless anger shook him.

"Oh God," he sobbed. "God, give me a sign. Tell me what you want me to do."

But nothing happened, and the man started to become aware of the numbing cold. He realized that, though he was warmly dressed, his limbs were probably frostbitten.

Despair hung heavy inside him as he saw a dead fetus lying in the middle of a cold empty room, no one caring. . . .

Oh please, God, please.

And then from deep inside he felt the sound coming up from his abdomen, and through his chest, and then hissing white hot from his lips. His eyes burned in the darkness and he uttered a language he had never heard but that he knew: The language of tongues.

"Jakom, hebredo, lackago, jutlcko—freedong ladoy!"

And then, in an instant, the man was covered with gooseflesh, and he felt a warmth like he had never felt before. He was sweating. He pulled off his coat and dropped it to the ground.

He reached his arms toward the heavens. Tears of joy spilled from his eyes.

God reached down from the heavens and touched the man on his shoulder, and God spoke to him:

3

"Go," God said, "and stop them."

A door inside the man opened up. The door of a furnace, that glowed white hot.

He would do it.

CHAPTER 2

Ivette Gonzalez was tired. She was looking forward to leaving for the day. It was now a quarter to five: she had been behind her desk at the J & L Clinic since a quarter to eight in the morning.

But it was more than just the time involved. It was the patients, the whole scene. It had seeped into her brain, and she didn't like it.

When she had first started the job two years earlier she thought that it wouldn't be that bad, particularly since the pay was quite good—seven dollars an hour plus time and a half for overtime.

But she was not ready for the parade of people coming through the door.

First, there were the nervous types. The girls who would sit in the waiting room and try to read—but couldn't. They had no attention span at all. Their eyes would constantly be flitting this way and that.

Ivette felt sorry for them, and she hadn't gotten used to it.

Then there were the young ones. Little girls thirteen and fourteen who were brought in by their mothers or fathers.

And sometimes they came in alone.

Then there were the old ones. The women in their thirties or maybe forties who made a mistake—and had to do something about it.

Then there were the white college girls, the ones who

came down to J & L because they were cheaper than all the other clinics.

The worst were what Ivette thought of as the pigs. These were the women who came back every five or six months. Abortion wasn't a medical thing for them, it was a method of birth control. They fucked their boyfriends, a baby formed, and then they got rid of it. They felt nothing for the baby; it was an inconvenience.

And it didn't cost them shit. Welfare paid.

Ivette hated those women.

But there were also the women who needed abortions for medical reasons. Ivette felt best about them, but they were still depressing. Most women just didn't want to have to give up their babies.

There was distrust on both sides: people who wanted to have abortions done had to pay in cash or certified check up front. One of the doctors had said that it was a "cash and uncarry" business.

Since four o'clock, Ivette had been doing paperwork. Normally, no operations were done after three o'clock.

The last patient of the day was in Recovery. She would be out in another ten minutes. Maybe, Ivette thought, she could get out a little earlier than she normally did, six o'clock.

The clinic was located on Tremont Avenue off Webster in a very bad neighborhood, so the door—a heavy metal one—was kept locked at all times. The junkies in the neighborhood were not above holding up the clinic. Ivette was sure they knew the patients paid in cash; they certainly knew the clinic had drugs they could use or sell.

She was in the process of clearing her desk when the front-door buzzer sounded.

It was, Ivette thought, a little early for the armored car that picked up the cash every day. That was another thing. There was no safe on the premises. The junkies would somehow have gotten into that.

She got up from behind her desk and went to the

door. There was a viewing eye there. She looked through.

Standing there was a very well dressed man. He was carrying a briefcase. He was smiling.

Ivette hesitated, then opened the door.

"Can I help you?" she said.

"Yes, my, uh, girl was supposed to be coming in today at three. I was supposed to meet her here but I got stuck in traffic."

"What's her name?"

"Joan Bilodeau."

Ivette's brow screwed up.

"Doesn't ring a bell," she said. "Come on in. Let me look at the log."

The man followed her in and she closed the door behind them.

She looked in the log. She was sure the name wasn't there. It wasn't.

"I'm sorry," she said, leafing through the pages to the next day's appointments. No luck there, either.

Now the man looked puzzled.

"God. Is there an L & J? Maybe I got the letters backward."

"I don't know."

"I better call her house."

"You can use this phone if you want."

"Oh, thank you very much."

Ivette got the man an outside line. He dialed a number with just a trace of difficulty because he was wearing gloves.

The phone rang a long time, and no one answered.

"God, I screwed this up," he said. "I'll just have to go over to her house."

Ivette nodded.

The man stopped and picked up his case, which he had put down.

"I wonder," he said, "if you have a bathroom I could use before I go."

"Oh sure," Ivette said, "it's right down that hall. First door on the right."

"Thank you," the man said. He went down the hall and she idly watched as he found the bathroom and went inside.

A few minutes later, he was on his way out the door.

"Thank you very much," he said.

"I hope you find your girlfriend," Ivette said.

"Yes, so do I."

Then he was gone, and Ivette locked the big metal door behind him.

CHAPTER 3

As she danced to "Twist and Shout," Jeanie Ryan felt like the music was *inside* her body. In a way it was. The music coming from the four-piece band only a few yards from where she was dancing was so loud it vibrated inside her lungs.

Jeanie's partner on the dance floor was her boyfriend, Bobby O'Rourke. Like her, he just loved to dance, something that was not too easy in the Bronx anymore for people who were white. Most Bronx bars where you could dance were black or Hispanic, and as an evening wore on—and booze and drugs flowed—things could get hairy for a pretty white girl with blond hair and a good body. Hairy for her, and hairy for whomever was with her.

So Jeanie and Bobby either went to Paddy's, The Duck, or Maguire's, which all were within walking distance of one another. The spicks and niggers knew that they were not welcome at any of those clubs.

Tonight they were at Paddy's, on Kingsbridge Road off the Grand Concourse.

Jeanie, who was an information operator for the telephone company, liked an audience, liked to let go. And she was a terrific dancer. Her legs were slim but well toned from her years on the track team at high school . . . and she was only twenty.

Bobby was a good dancer, too, but not as good as Jeanie. Though muscular, he didn't have her coordination; he didn't even have her wind. She really had endurance, and though Bobby was Jeanie's age, he sometimes felt a lot older.

Bobby liked it when people watched them dancing, and he also liked other guys looking at Jeanie and then looking at him with envy. He and Jeanie had been going out since they were both thirteen and in St. Barnabas Grammar School. Bobby knew that he loved her even more now than he did the first day he saw her. Jeanie had character. Bobby had seen that more than once, most especially over the last few years when her mother died of cancer and Jeanie took care of her the whole time.

To Bobby, Jeanie was the complete woman. He would notice other women, but that was about it. He could have the most beautiful girl in the world fall desperately in love with him, and it would mean no more to Bobby than rain on a window.

They planned to get married in two years. By then Bobby, who worked in Local 6 with his father, would be a journeyman plumber; right now he was a beginner. As his father had explained, "Your level of know-how at this point only requires you understand two things: shit runs downhill, and payday is Friday."

In three years, though, Bobby and Jeanie would be able to put a down payment on a house. Occasionally, on a weekend, they would drive to Jersey or Staten Island and look at houses.

They danced a slow dance, and then sat down at their table in the back. Tonight they were out with another couple, Jerry Rooney and Edna Gaughran, but they definitely didn't need other couples to have fun with.

They could have a lot of fun, and always had, just being with one another.

In fact, Bobby thought, he couldn't wait to get Jeanie alone tonight. Two months earlier he had moved out of his parents' home in Lynbrook and she had moved out of a city apartment to a private home up on Mosholu Parkway, which was not too far from the bar. The parkway was a broad road that ran though a park and somehow functioned as a moat that predators, who stayed south of the parkway, didn't cross.

The freedom of being in a room with one another to do whatever they wished had driven both of them crazy with a desire for sex. It had been nonstop.

Around midnight, Bobby and Jeanie began exchanging looks; it was time to leave. It was time to do something about the passion that had been building in them as the night wore on.

Around a quarter after twelve they said good night to Jerry and Edna and left.

It was a pleasant night, not too cold, a good night for walking.

But not in this neighborhood, they knew, unless you carried small arms and knew karate. Both Bobby and Jeanie knew the nickname for the area: Precinct Siberia.

They only had to walk a short distance from the bar to Bobby's car, which was parked about twenty-five yards up the block.

He had two cars, but only drove the bomb, a 1973 Mustang, in and around this neighborhood. It was less likely to be stolen than his better car, a 1958 black Chevy. He had restored that car to perfection and kept it parked in his mother's garage.

Bobby had a chain holding down the Mustang hood, so the local spicks couldn't make off with his battery.

Neither Bobby nor Jeanie had any fear. Neither figured there was much danger. All they had to do was yell—help would be surging out of Paddy's in seconds.

Within a minute, they were in the car with the doors locked. They started necking.

Another minute later, Bobby wrenched free.

"We gotta stop this," he said, rearranging his member, which was so hard it was almost painful, "or we'll give people a show."

Jeanie laughed, but she felt just like Bobby. She was all warm and wet.

Bobby started up the car, and a moment later they were moving north toward Mosholu Parkway.

They did not see the car, well down the block, that started to follow them immediately after they drove away.

CHAPTER 4

The man who was following them liked the idea of stalking. It was a good feeling, a very good feeling, like he was a lion in the bushes by a water hole, waiting for prey to come down to drink. It filled the man with a sense of excitement, and sexual power. As he travelled after them now he was half erect. His nostrils flared, and his eyes half closed as he contemplated what he was going to do.

He kept well back. It was only as they got closer to Stebbins Avenue that the man, who was driving a Blazer, carefully closed the gap. He wanted to be sure to be nearby when they parked.

Ten minutes after they left Paddy's, Bobby O'Rourke parked the car. He wasn't noticing much of anything himself, just the tremendous sensuality of Jeanie, and the fact that soon they were going to be making frantic love.

Neither Jeanie nor Bobby noticed the car that pulled

in and parked some thirty yards down the block. At that time they were arm in arm, on their way up the stairs to the porch. Twice they stopped and kissed on the way.

The man, who was short and muscular, made his way quickly toward them.

In his left hand he carried a small overnight bag containing various paraphernalia. In his right hand was a ski mask that he would momentarily slip on.

Jeanie and Bobby stopped on the porch to engage in a long, loving kiss. They did not hear or see the figure who slowly and silently—he wore soft-soled shoes—climbed the stairs beneath them. When they did, it was too late.

He said nothing when he got on the porch.

It was Jeanie who noticed him first.

"Bobby," she said, her voice tinged with fear. She had spotted the ski-masked man, and the gun in his right hand.

Bobby looked—and saw the gun. His immediate impulse to react was stifled. Guns did that.

"Anybody here?" the man asked.

"No," Bobby said.

"Inside," the gunman said. His voice was soft, but menacing. He was completely in control.

Bobby fished the key out of his pocket and opened an outside door that led to a small foyer and an inside door.

The man stood in the doorway as Bobby opened the inside one.

Bobby had a little trouble with the door. The light wasn't the best and his hand shook. But finally he got the key in and turned the cylinder.

"Inside," the man said.

They went inside. The man followed, the gun levelled all the way, and closed the door behind them.

Bobby and Jeanie had stopped. They didn't know what to do next.

"I live upstairs," Bobby said.

"Go," the man said.

Bobby and Jeanie walked up the stairs, Bobby in the lead, Jeanie behind. The man watched Jeanie. He liked the way her flesh pushed against the satin dress as she climbed, filling and tightening it. He was almost fully erect.

"Into the bedroom," the man said when they were on the second floor.

Jeanie had tears in her eyes. Bobby saw her. He was scared—but pissed. He would have to do something, but only when the time was ripe.

Bobby led Jeanie and the man down the narrow hall to the bedroom. They went inside. The man closed the door behind him.

"Get down on your stomachs," the man commanded.

Bobby knew that if he was going to do something, it would have to be now.

Jeanie, sobbing deeply, was getting on her stomach when Bobby acted. He made a movement as if to go down, but sprung at the man with all his strength and fury, trying to knock the gun away and at the same time smash his fist into the gunman's face.

But the gunman was as quick as a boxer. He evaded the rush and brought the gun up into Bobby's face with quiet ferocity. It made a terrible thumping sound, and Bobby was semiconscious by the time he flopped to the floor.

Jeanie had started to scream, but the man spit out, "Shut up or die."

Jeanie shut up. Control and power revved through the man's body like an engine at high speed. His penis was so hard it throbbed and was almost painful.

With practiced efficiency, he put the overnight bag on the floor and unzipped it.

From the bag he took out a pair of handcuffs. He placed the gun on the floor for a moment and pulled Bobby's hands behind his back and cuffed him. Bobby moaned.

The man went back to the bag and extracted a straight

razor. He flicked it open and shoved the gun down inside his pants.

Jeanie didn't see it because she was lying on her stomach.

He went over to her and roughly rolled her over.

Her eyes widened in total terror.

"You die if you disobey me," the man said. His voice was thick.

He reached down with one hand and grabbed the top of her dress. Using the razor, he cut it lengthwise as if it were butter, then used the razor to sever her bra and panties. He pulled all the clothing off and threw it aside as if it were no more important than wrapping on a package.

He dropped to his knees, straddling her chest. He unzipped his pants and pulled his erect member out. He lowered himself, grabbed her face roughly, and shoved himself into her mouth. Tears flowed from her eyes as he pulled her rhythmically onto him by her hair. She made choking sounds.

Abruptly, he stopped. He pulled the gun from his pants and laid it on the floor. He pulled his pants down and slid down her body.

Roughly, he entered her, and she sobbed in pain. She was dry. He drove himself into her ferociously. As he did, he glanced over at Bobby, whose eyes were open. He was crying.

The man stayed on her for five minutes, until she had nearly lost consciousness. He was proud of his ability to control orgasm.

Without ejaculating, he got up, went over, and straddled Bobby. He took the razor from his pocket.

He flicked it open, reached down, grabbed Bobby by the belt, and pulled him partly off the floor.

In one deft swipe he severed Bobby's belt, pants, and underwear. He dropped to his knees, and lay the clothing back as if he were unfolding a blanket.

He reached over and from the bag took out a jar of Vaseline. Bobby could see what he was going to do and struggled. The man smashed him in the face with his fist; blood spurted from his nose. Jeanie watched. Her eyes were dead. She was going into shock.

The man entered Bobby roughly, and drove at him with powerful strokes as deeply as he could. He heard the moans, and through the haze of lust he glimpsed the dead-eyed stare of the girl.

He was in full control, powerful, he wanted to hurt, hurt, hurt. He was doing just that.

He withdrew from Bobby. He was ready.

In a moment, he had dropped down on the girl's chest again. She was pliable, dead meat, but she resisted slightly when he stuck it into her. Ten seconds later he ejaculated.

He was master of the universe.

CHAPTER 5

Danny Parilli hated the Jericho Multiplex theater.

It was always so fucking crowded.

First, to get into the joint you had to stand on long lines, and half the time you didn't know what line you were on.

Second, everybody was so fucking rude. They would knock you over to get from one place to the other. A couple of times he had been tempted to break someone's face, but he was with Janet, a girl that his mother's friend had introduced him to, and he didn't want to make a bad impression.

They'd probably shoot you, Danny once thought, if you started to fight. The guards wore 9 mm automatics. Christ, what a fucking movie theater, where they had fucking guards wearing guns.

The whole thing reminded him of an airport. Next

thing you know to get into the place you'll have to empty your pockets and get your ass x-rayed.

Still, Danny went to the Jericho, because it usually had all the good movies. Probably paid off somebody.

It was Saturday night, and Danny was taking Janet to see the new Chuck Norris flick.

He had seen 'em all, and loved them. The guy was amazing. He was in his forties, but he was in great shape. Danny bet Norris could still beat most of the guys on the American Karate Club tour.

They saw the ten o'clock show. Danny would have liked to have taken her to an earlier one, or a later one when it was less of a madhouse, but she didn't like the early show and she worked in a bagel store on Sunday morning. She had to get up early.

One thing he had done to impress her was to drive his "horse." This was his twin-stack, thirteen gear, 450 hp tractor, called an eighteen-wheeler because it could haul trailers that totalled that many wheels. It was a Peterbilt, the Caddie of tractors, and he had customized it with chrome inside and out—chrome even on the gear knobs—and also had installed plush leather upholstery. Danny was quite proud of it.

The tractor was big and towered over anything around it, so when Danny and Janet came out of the movie he saw immediately that it was not where he had parked it. The steps in front of the theater were elevated, so he had a good view of the field. Feeling his heart hammering, he scanned the entire area.

Janet, a short, pretty, slightly overweight blonde, looked up at Danny. She could tell something was wrong.

"What's the matter?" she said.

"My rig," Danny said. "My—" He almost said "fucking." " —rig is gone."

"Are you sure?"

Danny did not answer. He was suddenly taking the steps two at a time.

Janet started after him and a moment later her heart

15

lurched. Crossing the area in front of the theater, Danny had almost gotten hit by a passing car.

Janet followed him across the lot, pausing first to make sure traffic wasn't coming.

The lines of cars were endless, and for a few minutes Janet lost sight of Danny. Then he appeared again.

When he got close, she could see that his face was mottled and though the night was cold—steam was coming out of his nose and mouth—he was sweating.

"It's gone," he said, "gone. Somebody stole it." His voice was reedy, close to breaking.

"Let's report it," Janet said.

Janet followed Danny as he walked rapidly back to the theater. He approached one of the uniformed guards, a black-haired Hispanic whose bulk pushed out against his dark blue uniform.

Danny told him what had happened.

The Hispanic was expressionless.

These people, Danny thought, are fucking subhuman.

"Come with me."

Danny and Janet followed him as he threaded his way through the crowded lobby, then around to a hall.

He opened a gray door and Danny and Janet followed him inside.

It was the Jericho Multiplex's version of Security Central. There were a couple of desks in the brightly lit, smoke-filled room and a bank of black and white TVs that monitored something.

The Hispanic went up to a jacketless guy sitting at one of the desks.

Danny could feel his heart still pounding. It was more than his rig that had been stolen. It was his livelihood. The day after tomorrow he was scheduled to deliver a load of frozen chicken to Hammond, Indiana. How was he going to do that?

But it was even more than that. Somehow Danny felt defiled, like he had been butt-fucked.

16

And it was very embarrassing. He figured he would have to get a ride home from his brother or else take a cab.

An hour later, Danny, alone now—his brother had picked them up and then dropped Janet home—was in the Third Precinct of the Suffolk County police department.

Danny thought it amazing, in a way. He was so excited about the loss of his truck, and the cop taking his statement at the desk—a heavyset guy with glasses who typed very slow—didn't seem to give a shit. Why the fuck should he? It wasn't his truck.

After the statement was complete, Danny signed the form.

"Has this ever happened at the Multiplex?" he asked.

A slight smile played around the cop's lips.

"It's right near the expressway. Niggers can come out from the city, steal the vehicle, and be back in the city in forty-five minutes. Yeah, it's happened. They call the Multiplex parking lot 'Jericho Ford.'"

Danny felt his stomach lurch.

"How good are the chances of me getting my truck back?" Danny said.

"Only about thirty-five percent of all vehicles are recovered. If this stays on the road we should find it fast, though. I'll have it on the wire soon."

"You mean because it's big and all."

"Yeah, but it's unlikely. That'll probably go right to a chop shop."

Danny looked at him. "You don't care, do you?"

"I'd like to get it back for you."

"But you don't seem to give a shit."

"You're insured, aren't you?"

"Yeah, but that's not the fucking point."

The cop got up and walked away and Danny left the station. He knew that unless he had a great deal of luck the rig was gone. Unless he could think of something else.

But he could not think of anything else. He could only hope that the cops could find it. It made him sick to think they probably wouldn't.

CHAPTER 6

José Rodriguez didn't like the idea of shopping in Garcia's Bodega, which was on Tremont off the Concourse. But he didn't have much choice on this Friday night. He had gotten paid but hadn't had a chance to cash his check, and he only had a few dollars on him. Garcia would give credit to Rodriguez, but he viewed Garcia as a hustler, just as bad as any white *maricón* ripping off Hispanic people.

But Rodriguez's new baby, Hector, didn't care about that—as long as he came home with the Similac.

As Rodriguez walked, he glanced idly down the block toward Anthony Avenue. It was almost seven o'clock, dark, but the corner street lamp illuminated the scene quite well.

There were a couple of niggers doing business. There was always somebody there. The Man had swept it every now and then but it didn't do no good. Ten minutes after The Man left the deals were being done again.

Rodriguez wondered where it would all end. He had grown up in *el barrio* and had sort of gotten used to the murder and mayhem that swirled around him, but now that he had a family of his own he worried. He didn't want his own babies to have to grow up in all this bad shit.

Rodriguez didn't think they would. He worked in the DMV in the city, and he and his wife, Ida, had been saving for five years to buy a house on Long Island, either in Brentwood or Islip, where there were a lot of Spanish, or farther east, where it was cheaper.

They had seven thousand dollars saved and would be able to put even more into the account next month. Rodriguez had received another promotion, which automatically carried an in-step increase, and he would be bringing home a fatter check.

He knew, too, that things might get dramatically better for PRs after the next election. The PRs were just at the point where they could put in a Spanish mayor rather than the usual Jew, Italian, or Irishman. A black had made it; why not a PR? Though Rodriguez was under no illusions about a PR mayor: he would be a politician before he was a Puerto Rican.

Most of the stores that lined Tremont were closed and had corrugated metal doors pulled down over them. A few years ago many of the stores would stay open pretty late, but then when crack came into big use they closed because the crack heads would congregate in them, and if something wasn't nailed down it was in danger of being stolen.

There were only two stores open down Tremont: Garcia's and La Mirada Cuchifritos Restaurant on the corner opposite where the niggers were doing business.

Both Garcia and the guy who ran the restaurant—Rodriguez didn't know his name—were crazy. They had been held up three or four times each, but it was the robbers who were at risk, not those guys. Both Garcia and the other guy carried licensed guns and Garcia had shot up one guy so bad he had almost died.

But Rodriguez had no doubt in his mind that one day Garcia and the other guy would be shot, maybe killed. Crack heads didn't care about nothing, least of all guns.

The black dudes went off the corner and then the street was empty except for an occasional passing car. The reason was the cold. It was only about twenty degrees out, and there was a wind. Rodriguez was a long way from the white beaches of San Juan.

The J & L Clinic was about halfway down the block, on the other side of the street. Like the other stores, its front was protected with a corrugated metal door.

Rodriguez figured it wouldn't be one of the places picketed by the right-to-life movement.

He would have smiled if his face had not been a frozen mask. The right-to-lifers, he thought, would be afraid to come into the neighborhood.

He had just looked away from it when the blast occurred, a sound so loud that Rodriguez yelped and went down to the street, his heart suddenly going a mile a minute.

Ten seconds later, he looked, trying to detect where the sound had come from, though he had more or less figured it out right away: the clinic.

He knew he better get to a phone.

CHAPTER 7

Bronx Central was one of the busiest hospitals in the city. Every single day a resident spent in Emergency at Bronx Central was equivalent to five days at a normal hospital. The citizens of Precinct Siberia were constantly doing one another bodily harm by means of guns, knives, clubs, corrosive liquids, bows and arrows, Mace, chopsticks, you name it.

Poor people were generally sicker than the rest of the populace, and were subject to diseases like plague and leprosy that other hospitals never saw. There were more AIDS victims in the area, and many of the women who were pregnant never received any prenatal care, and wound up giving birth, after a hectic ride in the back of a police car, on some gurney inside Emergency. Or in the police car itself. One old Irish hairbag of a cop had delivered seventeen babies in the back of a squad car.

Part of the standard equipment of the emergency ward was a so-called "rape kit," a small box containing all the equipment necessary for gathering evidence from a rape victim. There were swabs for taking specimens from the cavities of the victim, a comb for gathering hair samples—pubic hair was often exchanged during sex—and various other items for collecting specimens. Instructions were also included on how to use the kit.

Dr. Simon Prather, who worked Emergency at Bronx Central, did not need to read the kit instructions. He knew them as well as the alphabet.

It was Prather who examined Bobby O'Rourke and Jeanie Ryan when they were brought into the hospital in the wee hours of the morning.

As much as he had seen, and as much as he knew, it occurred to Dr. Prather nonetheless that the crime here was unusual even for Siberia: a couple had been raped. It was, as the cops might say, a distinctive MO.

The man, except for the trauma to the rectum, where a few blood vessels had been broken, was in fairly good shape. He had no concussion, lucky considering how hard he had been hit.

But his psyche was in bad shape. He was deeply depressed and ashamed.

Jeanie Ryan, the female victim, was in much better shape emotionally and physically. Dr. Prather felt that she would be fine, ultimately, but he wondered about Bobby O'Rourke. Only time would tell.

Ray Long and Kenny Garrido were in the radio car that responded to the 911 call from Bobby O'Rourke. Upon arrival at the scene, they had immediately called an ambulance, and then had called the desk at the Five Three to report the crime. The desk "Lou" had immediately called Barbara Babalino, a detective second grade who, with the other two female officers in the station, handled all rape squeals.

It had been learned the hard way that female detectives were often much better on rape investigations than men.

Barbara was particularly suited for the job.

She was sensitive, insightful, and had, in fact, wanted to be a psychologist before she went on the job. She had a reputation for being able to get facts from witnesses and victims where other cops had failed.

Jeanie Ryan told Barbara everything she remembered, her recitation broken only by an occasional sob.

There was a lot of detail, but not much helpful detail on who the perp might be.

He was described as short, muscular, and white.

He wore tight black gloves which he never took off.

He never took his ski mask off, but Jeanie thought his eyes were brown.

She described the gun well enough so that Barbara could be fairly certain it was a 9 mm.

There was nothing extraordinary about his voice.

"Can you remember anything at all distinctive about him?"

"Not really," the young woman said.

"Did he steal anything from you or Bobby?"

"No. He could have. We had some stuff in the room, a TV and VCR, but he didn't take anything. He even could have taken our money, but he didn't try. We had a couple of hundred dollars between us."

The questioning only took about twenty minutes, and then Jeanie and Bobby O'Rourke left the hospital.

Barbara drove back to the station.

It was, she thought as she drove, a very unusual MO. She had been handling rapes in Siberia for four years now, and this one was different. She had never encountered a *couple* being raped, though she had heard of a case out west. She would check that out, though her recollection was that the perp had been nailed and was in jail. She would put it on the wire here to see if anyone else had any similars.

Barbara Babalino was not the kind of a cop who could

become inured to human suffering, thought she had tried to a degree. This case bothered her, and she felt sorry for the young girl and the guy.

A rape—any rape—was like setting off a bomb in the psyche. It did tremendous damage to the victim and could affect relationships for years to come. Deep therapy could be required; its success was not assured.

One thing Barbara knew she could do. Catch the perp. She would do her damnedest to do that.

CHAPTER 8

Joe Lawless, felony squad commander at the Five Three, passed the desk of Sergeant Roy Fletcher, the oily aide-de-camp of Captain Warren G. Bledsoe, the CO. Unlike most of the other cops, Lawless did not stop at the desk to be cleared by Fletcher, who everyone knew was a sniveling little bastard who enjoyed exercising as much power as he could. Lawless simply tapped twice, then opened the door of the frosted glass corner office and went in.

Fletcher's face reddened but he said nothing. Lawless scared him, if for no other reason that Bledsoe didn't scare Lawless, as he did most cops. Lawless was a maverick, and when you looked into his hard, light blue eyes you just never knew how far he would go.

Lawless closed the door behind him.

Bledsoe, who was sitting behind the desk, had looked up as Lawless had come in. The captain, who was bald and had heavy eyebrows, was always on one diet or the other. He did not like Lawless, and he knew Lawless did not like him. But Bledsoe knew that he needed Lawless, because as much as he did dislike him, he knew also that he was a very good cop. He got cases cleared and helped keep the brass off his ass.

Lawless stopped in front of the desk. There was no greeting by either man.

"What'd you find out about that clinic bombing?" Bledsoe asked.

"Nothing much. The bomb squad says it was two M–80s wired to a clock. That's the equivalent of about a half a stick of dynamite. No one was hurt, and the only damage was the trash can the bomb was in and some smoke damage to the bathroom."

"Any leads?"

"The receptionist said a guy came in at about five o'clock, said that his girlfriend was supposed to have an appointment. The receptionist didn't find the woman's name for an appointment. The man said maybe he made a mistake. So he asked to use the bathroom before he left. That was likely the guy who placed the bomb."

"Description?"

"Dark hair, mustache, glasses."

"Did you make up a composite?"

"Why?"

"You want to collar him, don't you?"

"Yeah, but we have other priorities. The homicides are still coming in at 1.5 a week."

Bledsoe's eyes went flat for a moment. Son of a bitch, he thought. There was always a nasty edge to everything Lawless said to him.

"Well, we have to make him a priority now. The mayor got a note from the perp—in fact, two notes."

Bledsoe picked up two slips of paper from his desk and handed them to Lawless.

"He got the bottom one about three weeks ago, but he never showed it to anyone. The other one he got yesterday."

Which, Lawless thought, was the day after the bombing.

The notes were Xerox copies. Both notes were typed.

Lawless read the first.

Dear Mayor:

As you may or may not know, there are butcher shops all over the Bronx. They don't sell meat, and they don't sell frankfurters. What they sell, Mayor, is death. Death to all the *little babies that will never walk on God's Green Earth*.

These abortion mills have killed thousands of babies, but let this letter be a warning. Unless you see to it that they are shut down within two weeks, one or more of these death houses will be bombed.

Believe me. It's up to you. You better do something or you are going to be badly embarrassed.

Yours,
M. God's helper

Lawless looked up.

"Why didn't we see this?"

"Who the fuck knows. They didn't send it. They didn't even send copies to the clinics. They fucked up."

Lawless read the second note.

February 15

Dear Mayor,

Didn't I tell you that if you didn't see that those death houses were closed down I would bomb one?

I guess you didn't believe me.

Do you believe me now?

Maybe you do, but maybe you're not worried because I set off such a little bomb.

Don't count on that.

I am going to be watching the papers. If I don't see the clinics shut down I am going to set off another bomb. But it will be a lot bigger than the first.

It's all in your hands, Mayor.

Yours,
M. God's helper

Lawless looked at Bledsoe. Bledsoe said, "I not only got these notes delivered by pouch, but Assistant Chief Flynn called me to express the commissioner's concern. I don't give a fuck if this fuck blows the city apart, but I don't want him doing it here."

Lawless felt something hot surge inside him. He said, "I'll look into it. Can I take these notes?"

Bledsoe nodded.

"By the way," Bledsoe said, "before you do anything that might risk media exposure of this, check it out with me."

Lawless barely nodded and was gone.

CHAPTER 9

After leaving Bledsoe's office, Lawless climbed the worn, ribbed metal stairs to the second floor of the station and went into the felony squad room. This was a large room painted bile green like most of the station house, and filled with battered metal desks on which were relatively ancient typewriters and black phones. In one corner was a coffee maker and against one wall was a big chalkboard. There was a single window in the room, a dirty barred affair that framed part of the brick wall of an adjacent tenement, the only wall still standing.

"Gee," one of the squad members had said once, "it kills the view."

No one was in the squad room. Usually, very few people were—the populace kept them too busy. They were only in the rooms to write reports or attend brain-trust meetings on big cases.

Lawless poured himself a cup of black coffee and sipped it. Good. During the years that he had been at the Five Three—five years now—coffee quality in the squad room had definitely deteriorated. It had gotten to the point where, even freshly made, it had not tasted good. After a day sitting in the glass urn, it was "ready for the battery," someone once said.

But a new detective named Paige—who had since been transferred—had done some research and had found that aside from being made wrong, the biggest reason the coffee tasted bad was that the coffee maker didn't have a heating element that got hot enough. You really needed a good quality machine with a good heating element.

Then, an opportunity to get a machine presented itself when the feds seized a crack house on the fringes of the precinct. Among the contents was a Bunn coffee maker, which got "legs," as they say, and walked into the squad room.

Coffee quality had definitely improved.

Lawless sat down at one of the desks and leafed through a dog-eared copy of the Bronx Yellow Pages.

He found six abortion clinics, and he knew that at least one of the hospitals in the precinct, Bronx General, performed abortions.

He picked up the phone and made the first call.

"Manuel Clinic."

"This is Detective Lawless from the fifty-third precinct. May I speak with the director?"

"Oh . . . yes," came the startled reply.

A half a minute later, the director came on the phone. He identified himself as John Hernandez.

"May I help you?" he asked.

"I'm calling," Lawless said, "all the clinics in the Bronx to alert them to a possible danger of a bombing."

"Oh. I heard about I & L."

"Yes," Lawless said. "Tell your people to be extra careful about who they let in."

"Do you think I should hire a security guard?"

"That's up to you. Just be extra alert."

"Okay."

"Have you noticed anyone unusual around the clinic lately?"

"No."

"Good."

Lawless gave the clinic director his number and instructed him to call if anything suspicious occurred.

Lawless called the other clinics. He was able to get through to everyone except Bronx General; an administrative aide of some sort said they would call Lawless back.

Lawless said they should, soon—that the facility could be in danger.

He got himself another cup of coffee, lit another cigarette—he was trying to cut down and it was only his fourth all day—and called Fred Billericks, an agent with the Alchohol, Tobacco and Firearms Bureau.

He got right through.

"Hey Freddie. Joe Lawless. How you doing?"

"Good, Joe. How are you?"

"I'm fine. When did we last talk?"

"That Torres job?"

"I think so," Lawless said. The Torres job was easy to remember. Someone named Juan Torres had torched an old-people's home on Fordham Road and four people had died.

"What have you got?" Billericks said.

"A bomber. Did you hear about the J & L Clinic here? That was this guy."

"Sure, I heard of that. What's he doing now?"

"Threatening to make bigger bombs. I just want to get your input on the case."

"Name the time and place."

"It's kind of pressing."

"I'm supposed to leave for Kentucky tonight. Can you meet me at the airport? We can have a drink."

"Absolutely."

They arranged to meet at the TWA lounge at nine.

At ten after seven the security director at Bronx General called and Lawless filled him in on what was going on. The director, an ex-cop named Hannigan, thanked him and said he would beef up his force.

After Lawless hung up, he thought again of something that he had thought of from time to time as he made the calls.

This bomber business could leak to the press. If that happened he knew the mayor, an astute political animal, would want to know where the leak came from, and ultimately it would come back to him.

On the other hand, Lawless felt he had little choice. He had to do what he had to do.

Guiltily, Lawless allowed himself a fifth cigarette. Then he started to do some work on the other cases he had open.

CHAPTER 10

Lawless met Fred Billericks in the second floor lounge of the TWA terminal at JFK Airport at nine o'clock.

Almost all the tables were filled, even though it was a Monday night in a cold month, probably because lots of people didn't like to fly, and had to shore up their courage before they did.

Billericks hardly looked like an ATF agent. He was short, blond, muscular, and looked young for his age, which was forty-two. He looked more like a phys ed teacher. But he had been with the ATF for almost fifteen years, and during the last two years had headed the teams that had supervised three of the biggest bombing cases in America in the last decade. He was a very good cop.

After the waitress delivered their drinks, Lawless brought out copies of the notes received from the bomber.

"I just want to see if you have any experience with this guy," Lawless said, "and also give me your thoughts on what you think we're dealing with."

He handed the notes to Billericks.

Billericks wore glasses, but to read the notes he pushed them to the top of his forehead.

He read both twice.

"I have no familiarity with the person who wrote the notes, but I would say you're definitely dealing with a fanatic."

"You think so, huh?"

"Definitely. It has that aroma. People like this are the most dangerous—dangerous because they are fanatics, committed to a cause that's more important than themselves. I always think of guys—if it is a guy—like this in the same way I think of kamikaze pilots. I mean, no one wants to die. So it takes real dedication to throw down an inch of sake, climb into a plane, and fly off to your death. And people like this do it willingly. They glory in it."

Lawless felt a slight gripping sensation in his stomach. It was the same kind of feeling he had gotten when he read the notes. Now, Billericks had confirmed it.

"Do you remember that abortion clinic bombing a couple of years ago down in that little town outside Atlanta?" Billericks asked.

"Yes."

"I supervised the investigation—and nowhere did this type of fanaticism hit me more than on that case."

Lawless nodded.

"There were two young couples involved; both had been married within the last year. These were people for whom God was the center of their world. No, more than the center. He was everything. You'd go into their homes and there were religious statues and pictures everywhere, and they were always explaining life with this or that reference to the Bible, and they went to church every chance they could."

Billericks took a hefty belt of his beer. He glanced

at a clock above the bar. He had plenty of time.

"The thing was—is—that they think of themselves as instruments of God. There's no arguing with them, telling them that it's wrong to hurt people. They don't see it. They are absolutely convinced of the rightness of their position."

"Did anyone get hurt in that bombing?" Lawless asked.

"An old caretaker got his legs blown off—and died about a week later. Didn't bother these folks one bit. They had it all worked out in their heads. Said that it was God's will."

Billericks's jaw muscles worked.

"Scary, stupid, crazy . . . it's a problem."

"I'd like to get you involved."

"Okay. I'll be back in a few days," Billericks said, taking another swig of his beer. "What are you doing meanwhile?"

"I'm just getting started on it. I'm going to show the notes to some cops I know worked on bombers. Maybe I'll get lucky."

Billericks nodded.

"You can also use our computers if you want. Just see a guy named Al Miner and tell him I said it was okay."

"Thanks Freddie," Lawless said. "I appreciate that."

And he did. The ATF computers had all kinds of information in them about virtually everyone in the U.S. Cases had actually been solved by one man sitting at a computer, checking and cross-checking, and following an electronic trail to produce prime suspects—and perps.

Lawless and Billericks stayed at the lounge ten more minutes, then Billericks left to catch his flight. Lawless was glad this man was going to help.

CHAPTER 11

Barbara Babalino started knocking on doors the day after the double rape.

Fortunately, Barbara spoke Spanish, because most of the potential witnesses were Hispanic. If you spoke Spanish it was an indication of respect for their language and, by extension, respect for them.

Still, as she canvassed the building on Mosholu Parkway, she wasn't getting many results.

If anyone had seen something, he wasn't talking.

A couple of times men who answered the doors seemed interested in rape—raping Barbara.

In many of the apartments she found men who seemed perfectly capable of working, but who didn't and instead stayed home and collected welfare. Barbara was not particularly angry at that. People would say that such people ripped off the system, but Barbara knew they were ripping off themselves. As long as they depended on handouts for survival they were not going to get anywhere.

But what did piss Barbara off were the houses where she noticed only kids present—sometimes kids under a year. When she spotted this she would immediately stop what she was doing, hit the street, and make a call to the welfare people.

Barbara didn't want to let one of those kids die in a fire or choke or get electrocuted because its mother wasn't there.

Occasionally, a door would be opened by some elderly person, a non-Hispanic, an old Irishman or a Jewish woman. These were people trapped by economics, with no one to care for them, forced to spend the last years of their lives behind multiple-locked doors, scared to emerge. For them, going on the street was a very scary experience.

Once she had dissipated the original fears these people displayed, Barbara lingered as long as she could. She knew that these people were also very lonely, and in one of the cases, she stopped to have a cup of tea in an old Irish lady's apartment.

It was 1945 inside that room—the furniture, the pictures, the furnishings, everything. Barbara could well imagine that the woman's fantasies would transport her back to that time. It was certainly a better time than she knew now.

Within two days, Barbara had canvassed most of the homes in the area. No one admitted to seeing anything.

A couple of times Barbara sensed that a person might have noticed something, but was keeping quiet.

She made a note of these people. When she hit a dead end she would come back—and hit them harder.

Periodically, she would call in to the station house and speak to Joe Lawless. He was not thrilled in the least with the idea of Barbara canvassing the buildings alone, even though he was well aware that she could handle herself better than most men. He had tried to talk her into taking someone from the squad with her, but she wouldn't hear of it.

"It's broad daylight," she said, "and I think anyone who spots me is going to figure me for a cop. What would a young, well dressed white woman be doing in these buildings? They would have to know that I'm trouble."

Lawless was not impressed with her line of reasoning.

"You know how some of these people are," he said. "You meet some crack head and he won't care what you look like."

But Barbara was adamant about it. She could take care of herself.

At one point, Lawless gave up. She was not bull-headed, but once she was convinced of the rightness of

33

her position she was very difficult to dissuade. This independence and sense of individuality were the very qualities Lawless loved in her. Barbara Barbalino was her own person.

It was a good thing Lawless didn't see what occurred near the end of the second day that Barbara had been canvassing.

Inside the building she was in it was not broad daylight. The lights on the bottom two floors were missing—probably stolen—and as she came down the stairs, she could hear muffled voices on the lowest landing.

She went down the next flight of stairs, and then, suddenly, there was silence.

She had been able to hear whoever was downstairs, therefore they would be able to hear her.

Why had they suddenly stopped talking?

She had an explanation that she didn't like, and briefly considered going back up the stairs, across the roof, and down.

But she was a cop. If somebody was going to be mugged, she would rather it be her than one of those old people upstairs.

She was wearing a loose coat, and her snub-nosed .38 was in her right hand pocket, loose. As she walked down the stairs she listened intently and wrapped her right hand on the gun.

When she hit the landing, she could sense that someone was under the stairs, waiting to spring. Her pulse was racing, and she was coiled—ready for anything.

There was a cracked mirror mounted on one wall, and a quick glance there confirmed what she knew: there was someone under the stairs.

She considered pulling her weapon, but waited.

And a moment later exited the building without incident.

Outside, she went across the street. Fifteen seconds after she had left two black males, whom she estimated to be in their early twenties, exited the building.

They looked left to right—and spotted Barbara.

There was a moment of indecision on their part, and then they started walking east along Mosholu.

Barbara had no doubt that they were the people under the stairs. Why they hadn't attacked her she could only speculate. Maybe it was her body language, something that told them to beware, that this wasn't just some defenseless female they would be attacking.

Barbara told herself that next time she would concentrate on making herself seem more vulnerable, if she could.

At the end of the third day she had completed canvassing the buildings—with no luck. There were a few people she had to see who weren't in, but she didn't have high hopes.

She quit at about seven o'clock, then went back to the station house.

Barbara was one of the privileged few at the station house: she had her own office, albeit a tiny little thing that could barely accommodate a desk and two chairs. Fortunately, she was neat, so it stayed fairly livable. And it was cream colored, not bile green.

The office was unofficially known around the station as the " trauma room." It was where Barbara and Kate Sanders, another detective in the Five Three, would ordinarily do the interviewing of female victims.

Barbara called the desk to get her messages. She had half a dozen, including one from Joe. He said he would see her later tonight.

She knew that it would be very much later tonight. He was working on the bomber case with the ATF; he had told her they were pretty sure this guy was going to strike again.

There were five messages related to cases she was working on, including one from an assistant DA, Anna Romero. In a couple of weeks Barbara would have to testify in another rape trial. Going to court always involved a large expenditure of time, so she hoped she could make good progress on this case before her appearance.

There was one other call, this from a Lieutenant Bickford of the Second Squad in Huntington. She had no idea what it was about. She figured she would call in the morning.

She spent another hour at the station doing paperwork, then went home to the apartment she shared with Joe in the Pelham Bay section of the Bronx.

CHAPTER 12

Barbara Babalino was in the next morning at seven o'clock, an hour before her tour started. This week she would be on days and Sanders, the other female detective, on nights.

She managed to halve the pile of paperwork in an hour. She had a rule that was the secret to being so organized: if she picked up a piece of paper, she dealt with it.

Barbara felt good. Joe had gotten home at about one. She was just falling off to sleep—but had awakened to Joe's hard, warm, naked body pressed close to her, and they had made love for a half hour.

She and Joe had tentatively set their marriage date for June, and in a few weeks Barbara would start making formal plans. She wanted a big wedding, and so, surprisingly, did Joe. He was a bit on the shy side and tended to do things low-key, but he had readily agreed to this.

"The one thing I do demand," he said with his typical dry sense of humor, "is that we have an EMS unit at the church. I don't know if I can survive seeing you in a wedding dress. Sometimes when I see you dolled up

I feel a coronary coming on. Even when you're not dolled up you can do that to me."

Barbara smiled. Joe was such a romantic—in everything. At first you didn't see that about him, because he was such a streetwise cop and, like most of them, paranoid. But deep inside she always sensed that he was an idealist, who still believed that the world could be changed despite all he had seen, particularly during the last five years in Siberia.

She felt the same way. She had been on the job for eight years, and she certainly had developed a crust that she didn't have when she began. But deep down she still believed she could make a difference.

She loved Joe so, and was sure their marriage would work.

He had been married once before, but that didn't work because his wife really didn't understand what being married to a cop meant.

Barbara had also been married once before—to a young guy who turned out to be a drug addict and who eventually died.

She knew that female cops had a very high divorce rate, maybe one hundred percent, because of the "four to fours"—a four to twelve tour, followed by a twelve to four in bed with her partner.

But they would be all right. Once she had fixed on Joe, she had hardly even noticed other men.

At 8:30, Barbara called the Second Squad at Huntington and was transferred into the detectives' squad room.

She identified herself, and was connected to Detective Bickford.

"Yeah," Bickford said, "the squeal you got sounds like our Mr. Wrigley's."

"What do you mean?"

"This guy attacks couples. Somebody nicknamed him Wrigley's."

She got it—double your pleasure. Leave it to cops, she thought.

"How many do you have?"

"Two reported. Both in Huntington."

Barbara knew where that was: about forty miles out on the north shore of Long Island. She had gone out to the town a few times.

"How long ago?"

"One in November, one in December. Sounds like your guy. Both couples were young, white, both were followed to their apartments and were assaulted inside."

"Can I come out to see you?"

"Anytime."

"I'll come now."

"Bring your file, okay?"

"Sure."

Barbara left two hours later, after taking the statements of an elderly Hispanic woman whose home had been burglarized, and of an old black woman who had been mugged. Business as usual in Precinct Siberia.

CHAPTER 13

Barbara drove to Huntington in Joe Lawless's car. It was only about fifty miles from Siberia to the town, which was actually composed of a number of smaller towns, sprawled out over quite a bit of territory—ten square miles.

As Long Island towns went, Huntington was particularly nice looking. Hills, manicured lawns, water, bright and well-maintained homes. Peaceful.

Still, Barbara knew that there was something else beneath the surface of Huntington.

There was plenty of crime: burglaries, rapes, muggings, murders . . . it was just that there wasn't as much as in Siberia, and the people weren't as obviously bad off. Indeed, people in the suburbs generally had pretty good jobs, which kept them going.

But maintaining this life-style was the very thing that killed the kids of the suburbs, Barbara thought, in the same way, really, that the kids of Siberia died. Both groups were victims of neglect, only the good-looking houses and manicured lawns and well-tended landscaping, the appearance of health and normalcy, hid the sad underbelly: the kids on drugs, driving at high speeds and doing what they wanted to do.

Barbara had vowed one thing: when she had a child, she would throw in her papers. There was no way, she figured, that you could be a cop and raise a child. There was no way you could be anything but a mother and raise a child. It was a full-time job.

Barbara got to the Second Precinct in Huntington at about eleven o'clock.

As she entered the building, a one-story red brick structure, she hoped that Bickford would not be a jerk. Some cops from different jurisdictions would treat visiting cops like they had the plague, particularly if they were New York cops.

Barbara figured it was jealousy. The NYPD wasn't what it used to be, but there was no question in her mind that it was still The Finest.

The fact that she was a woman didn't bring cheers from most other cops either. Lots of them tended to look down their noses at her.

Still, Bickford had sounded fine on the phone. Very professional.

She waited at the front desk only a minute before Bickford came out.

Barbara got good vibes instantly. He was tall, paunchy, red-faced, maybe in his late fifties. He had blue, slightly protuding, typical cop eyes. They were always asking, Who have you ripped off, killed, or assaulted lately?

"Barbara?" he said, extending a big hand. "Jack Bickford."

Barbara smiled, shook his hand, and then followed him through a door adjacent to the desk.

He made small talk as she followed him through a series of halls and into a large office. For a moment, Barbara wondered how a squad detective could have such an office, then realized it wasn't his.

"This is the squad commander's office," Bickford said, "but he's out today. We can use it."

He went around and sat down behind the desk.

"Please sit. I pulled the files," he said, gesturing to two thick cream-colored files on the desk. "You can study them, if you like, and then we can talk. Or we can talk about them now."

"I think I'll study them first," Barbara said. She reached into her briefcase, which was sitting on her lap. "I brought my file on the Ryan assault for you to look at." She handed it across the desk to Bickford.

"Good," he said. "Thank you."

As Bickford was getting up to leave, Barbara stopped him with a question. "What's your sense of this guy?" she asked. "Is he going to trip up?"

Bickford looked at her. She could see the glimmer of respect in his eyes. He liked the question. It was one thing to read files and talk to witnesses and do all the other standard police work. But the instincts of an individual cop, particularly an experienced one, could be worth much more.

"He's a cutie pie," Bickford said. "Very careful. No one has seen him yet. He always wears a ski mask, never takes his gloves off."

"Did you investigate it hard?"

"We had a lot of people on it. Nothing. The only way we linked the two assaults was because the MO was the same."

Barbara nodded. "I'll read the files."

"Likewise," Bickford said.

"Thanks again."

He smiled and left the room, closing the door on the way out.

Barbara got up and sat down behind the desk. She glanced at the files.

On the cover was a tab that said KEENAN, NOVEMBER 15. The other said FREDA, DECEMBER 12.

She picked up the file on the earlier case and opened it.

CHAPTER 14

It had been a long, long haul for Frank Piccolo. The little man, a detective first grade in Siberia, had lost his partner, Eddie Edmunton, one hot summer night a year and a half earlier.

Edmunton, just finished with a decoy job, had stopped to question a dapperly dressed black dude driving a BMW. The guy turned out to be a member of one of the Jamaican posses and a drug dealer. Without warning he had stitched Edmunton with a Tech 9. Eddie was flatline before he reached the hospital.

Just like that there was no more Eddie, and from that moment on time stopped for Frank Piccolo. There was no yesterday, there was no tomorrow. Just now. The fucker who cut Eddie down must go. Piccolo did not think of whether he would live or die or quit the job or anything. The only reality was to nail the fucker who had killed Eddie.

Life without that had no meaning, no significance to Piccolo whatsoever.

For the sake of the Felony Squad commander, Joe Lawless, Piccolo had done nothing immediately.

Lawless knew how dangerous the little man ordinarily was. On the street those who knew him gave him a wide berth. But in this state, a state of mourning over his partner, he was like a walking can of gasoline.

Lawless wanted to save him—save his job, save his life. He had three reasons: he was a cop, he was in the squad, and he was a friend.

Piccolo had gone to California, walked along white beaches, and watched seagulls circle over an azure sea. He had wept for his buddy, his buddy Eddie who had died so young. Gone forever in the fucking rat-tat-tat of some motherfucking cheap gun.

And he had screamed—screamed from the agony of the white-hot anger that burned inside his guts.

But he had stayed in California, some nights drinking himself into a stupor, and once imagining that Eddie was in the room with him, sharing a glass of guinea red like he used to.

Then, Lawless had called him back. They had a lead. They pursued the lead down a twisting path that took Frank Piccolo halfway across the country, and then back to New York.

And then they had a name, and Piccolo restrained himself.

They set the dude up. The were going to make him fall. All nice and legal.

And then they discovered their main witness, dead and jointed in a dumpster, and the case flushed away, that quick, just the way Eddie had gone.

The shooter was free. He had closed all loose ends, pulled up the moat, no one could touch him.

But there was still one loose end. Its name was Frank Piccolo.

One day in early autumn Piccolo went out to Edmunton's grave and buried his shield beside it, because Piccolo figured he might not be coming back.

Then he took a flight to Kingston, Jamaica, and drove to Tivoli Gardens, where all the posses got their start, and found the bar where the shooter held court.

Less than twelve hours later Piccolo was on an Air Jamaica jet lifting out of Kingston, and the shooter was on a gurney in the Kingston morgue being opened up with a power saw.

The ME counted seventy-four separate entry wounds.

Lawless had read about it in the paper and instantly knew who the perp was, and so did many of the other cops in the Five Three, but no one said anything to anyone, and no one ever would. It has been said that cops are closer to other cops than to their wives. They are.

That event was the beginning of the road back for Piccolo. It was like he had been down, heard the count over him at seven, and managed to stagger to his feet before they counted him out.

He had gone back to the cemetery and talked with Eddie, and Eddie told him to stay a cop. So he did.

He got another apartment in the Bronx, and started a new pet collection. Before Eddie had been killed, he and Piccolo had shared an apartment with five unusual pets: a python, a monitor lizard, a tokay gecko, a boa constrictor, and a wolverine. But he had given them up, along with the apartment, following Eddie's death.

Piccolo's first new pet was a Tasmanian devil, which, he had heard, was second only to a wolverine in its ferocity.

The one thing Piccolo wanted was a new partner, but other cops at the precinct shied away from him. Piccolo had a way of getting into hot water, whether it was looking down the wrong end of a barrel or getting into a beef with the brass. Since most of the cops at the Five Three were considered misfits and had been sentenced to Siberia, they weren't anxious to get in trouble. The next stop was turning in the gun and shield.

Lawless did not assign Piccolo a partner. He understood that would be fruitless. If Piccolo didn't like the partner, he wouldn't last. It was that simple. Or if the guy didn't like partnering with Piccolo, that wouldn't work either, probably, though there were cop partners who hated each other but worked together like a Swiss watch.

Then along came Howard Stein, who was, like Piccolo, a mental case.

Stein was a kid from the Bronx who had grown up in the Arthur Avenue section and walked his first post in Harlem, shipped there because he had angered one of the instructors at the Academy. The brass who sent him there were hoping Harlem would chew him up and spit him back in pieces.

It didn't happen. Stein wasn't so easy to chew.

When he was growing up in Arthur Avenue, Stein had six fistfights with Italian kids, mostly because they got down and dirty about him being Jewish. He had the fifth fight when he was twelve, and there was a five year gap between that and his sixth and final fight. The sixth fight was with a guy who had just moved into the neighborhood and had not seen the first five fights.

Stein's father had. been a superintendent, and Stein had been pulling dumbwaiters since he was about six—with his left arm only. Thus, his left arm had developed like the left arm of Rod Laver, the championship southpaw tennis player from Australia; it had become huge, muscular, and thicky veined, while the right arm was relatively thin, veinless—human size.

Around Arthur Avenue he was known as "Thunderfist," and all six of his fights were one punch affairs. In Harlem he followed regulations and carried a baton, but he never used it. One swing of his fist was all that was necessary. If he connected, the fight was over.

It was his thunder-fist that got him to Siberia.

Incensed at a laughing defendant who had gotten a light sentence from a liberal judge, Stein had sidled up to the man as he was led out of court and fractured his jaw in four places.

Like Piccolo, Stein was a highly decorated police officer. And it was this, plus perhaps some perception by the brass that Stein would fight to the bitter end, that prevented his dismissal, though he was suspended for a month.

Stein and Piccolo got along instantly, and within a few days it became clear to Lawless that they would make good partners.

Piccolo agreed.

They now had been together about six months and were known on the street as Frankenstein, which more or less described their effect on bad guys.

The word triggered a strange, and maybe sick, thought in Piccolo. In the movies, Frankenstein was very difficult to kill, and Piccolo thought of it as a lucky name. He and Howie would be very hard to kill, too.

On a Friday afternoon in late February it was like old times in Frank Piccolo's apartment. There he was in the kitchen with his partner, polishing off a half gallon of cold guinea red, talking about this, that, or the other thing, occasionally hearing the Tasmanian devil stir in its cage.

Howie wasn't as talkative as Eddie had been, but it was nice just having him there listening—and occasionally he would say something.

Someday, Frank hoped, Howie would talk about his wife and two kids, who had left him. Frank knew that hurt Howie bad, but Frank knew also that to probe it directly would not be a good idea.

All in good time. He and Howie, he knew, were going to be together a long time.

Frank was talking about how to best use a sledgehammer in taking down a door when the phone rang.

Stein answered the phone on the kitchen wall. "It's for you, Frank."

Piccolo got on the phone.

"Uncle Frank, its Danny Parilli." Danny Parilli. He was his sister Veronica's son.

"Yeah Danny, how you doin'?"

"Bad, Uncle Frank, bad. Someone stole my rig and the cops can't find it."

"Give me details."

Parilli did. He told them how it was stolen from the Jericho Multiplex, how he had spoken with the security guards without result, and how the Suffolk cops didn't seem to care.

"How long ago this happen?" Piccolo asked.

"A week."

"Hey, Danny," Piccolo said, "it's probably gone. Unless a kid got it. You might find it then."

"That truck's my living," Parilli said.

"You were insured, right?"

"Yeah, but all that takes awhile. Anyway, it's my truck. You understand, right Uncle Frank?"

Piccolo understood. He had a 1975 Trans Am that he babied and took care of. If someone nabbed that, he would be heartbroken.

"Could you," Parilli said, "maybe look for it?"

"I ain't promising nothing," Piccolo said, "but I'll give it a shot. Let me write down some stuff."

Piccolo got a pad and pen and wrote down the details his nephew gave on the truck as well as the cops who were handling it.

"I'll be in touch," Piccolo said before he hung up.

Piccolo sat back down. He explained to Stein what had happened to his nephew.

"Sounds like a chop shop," Stein said.

"Probably," Piccolo said. "A new Peterbilt like that—it's either been chopped or on it's way to fucking Botswana."

They drank in silence.

"You going to give it a whack, Frank?" Stein said.

"Yeah," he said, "we got today and tomorrow."

It was true. Both men had come off what was technically an eight o'clock tour, though there were never any normal tours in the Five Three. They were not due in until the next night at midnight.

But Frankenstein was always on duty, acting out their

shared philosophy of breaking balls and making life as miserable as possible for bad guys, particularly dealers. They had a habit of showing up at random, a two-man TNT force in a neighborhood or housing project, and clearing the streets. They had a bad reputation.

"They ain't like regular cops," one dealer said. "Frankenstein'll motherfucking ice you just like that. They're motherfucking worse than us."

They finished their guinea red in silence.

CHAPTER 15

Neither Piccolo nor Stein had been to a movie in years—unless you counted the time Piccolo hid behind an air-conditioning duct in the old DeLuxe Theatre on East Tremont Avenue in an effort to nail a "prevert" who was accosting people. Cops didn't have time to go to movies. They had a twenty-four hour horror movie going on in Precinct Siberia.

The Jericho Multiplex, then, was something of a shock when Frankenstein showed up at around five in the evening the day Danny Parilli had called.

As they walked toward the theatre, Piccolo said, "This fucking place is huge. There's got to be space for five thousand vehicles here."

Stein, like the Suffolk cop, realized why it might be a popular place to steal vehicles. "This is three minutes from the highway."

"Yeah," Piccolo said, "you're right. But we'll go through the motions anyway, right?"

"Right."

Inside, the lobby was immense and basically empty, except for a uniformed black guy vacuuming the floor with a big machine. Stein asked him where the security office was and got directions to it.

They found it without a problem. The door was open. There was one uniformed security guard in the room, and he was sitting behind a desk that faced the door. He was on the phone. He was a young Spanish guy with long black hair.

He looked up when Piccolo and Stein came in. He had been smiling as he talked but his expression changed when he saw them.

"Yeah," he said.

Stein and Piccolo flashed their tin.

"We're from New York," Piccolo said, "looking into a truck theft."

The young guy nodded and went back to the phone. Piccolo and Stein assumed he was going to hang up and speak with them. They assumed wrong.

Two minutes later, the guy was still on the phone, and it was obviously not a business call. Not unless the business associate was named "Cookie" and made the guard smile and coo.

As they entered the third minute of waiting, Stein took off his jacket.

The young guy glanced at Stein's arm—stopped talking for a moment to marvel at it—then went back to his conversation.

It happened without warning.

There was a buffeting sound, and then the explosion as Stein's fist crashed through the half-inch Sheetrock wall, sinking totally out of sight.

The young guard dropped the phone with a clatter on the desk. "What the fuck . . . ?" he managed.

Stein withdrew his fist and drove it into the wall again.

Piccolo stepped forward and leaned across the desk. He did not have his teeth in and he smelled of guinea red. He had his normal look in his eyes—the elevator did not go to the top floor.

"How about a little fucking respect," he said. "A

little motherfucking, cocksucking courtesy?"

The guard had turned white.

"I gotta go," he said into the phone, and hung up.

Stein pulled his fist out of the wall. "We're police officers," he said, "and we deserve respect."

The guard's eyes flitted from one man to the other. "What do you want?"

Piccolo stood up straight. Stein stepped forward. The guard's eyes kept being drawn to Stein's huge, hairy rope-veined arm—the hand white with plaster, pieces of stuff on the fingers.

"You had a Peterbilt stolen out of here a week ago. We want to see the report on it," Piccolo said.

The guard stood up and went to a gray filing cabinet behind him. He leafed through, withdrew a paper, and handed it to Piccolo. He and Stein read it.

There was nothing much there, just the report of the theft and a note that it was referred to the Suffolk cops.

There was a Suffolk cop's name in the report: Herman Diaz.

"This all you got?" Stein said. "Did anybody see anything?"

"No. We don't do investigating on these. The cops do that."

"What do you mean 'on these'?" Piccolo asked. "You get a lot?"

"Yeah. At least one every two weeks."

"What?" Stein asked.

"What?"

"What kind of vehicles?"

"Mostly new cars. But this is the second truck in the last month."

Stein and Piccolo were thinking the same thing: the parking lot of the Jericho Multiplex was a candy store for thieves. The chances of Parilli getting his truck back were practically nil. With that kind of thievery they were not dealing with kids, they were dealing with pros.

Piccolo handed the report back to to the guard.

They turned to leave.

"Hey," the guard said, "what about the wall?"

Stein made a motion as if to blast the wall again, and both he and Piccolo roared. Then they were gone.

CHAPTER 16

Frankenstein was lucky.

Herman Diaz, the Third Precinct squad cop who handled Parilli's squeal, was in.

Diaz, a small, chunky guy with bad skin, spoke to them as they sat in the squad room at the SCPD Precinct, which had jurisdiction over the thefts at the Multiplex.

"There's an epidemic going on with these trucks," he said. "There have been five stolen in two months from the Multiplex, and all were less than thirty days old. There have also been six new car thefts. We've never had repeats like that. Definitely a pattern—the same guys are doing the thefts. And there's more to it than that."

"How so?" Piccolo asked.

"There's been a wave of these truck thefts in the tristate area. The five out here, some in Jersey, a couple in Connecticut, a couple in the city. This is a big ring operating. There's big money in these eighteen wheelers. Plus the increase in car thefts."

"How much?" Stein asked.

"They can bring in a hundred grand per if a chop shop takes 'em. I don't know how much if they get exported—maybe double that."

"You're talking about making two hundred thousand dollars, for how much effort?" Piccolo said. "A minute to steal it, and with little risk."

"And if they chop it, another hour," Stein added.

"A lot of money," Diaz said.

"How far have you gotten with your investigation?" Piccolo asked.

"Nowhere. These guys are slick."

"Do you see an inside job?"

"No," Diaz said, "the trucks come in from different states so far as I know. There's no insider pattern. Of the four stolen out here only two are from New York. Truckers traveling the Long Island Expressway stopped to see a movie. And trucks stolen in other states are also from different states."

"You said a couple were taken in the city."

Diaz leafed through some papers. "One was taken from the parking lot of the Market Diner on Forty-third and Tenth in Manhattan and the other was stolen off a street in the Bronx—Fordham Road and the Grand Concourse."

Frankenstein looked at one another and read one another's thoughts: Fordham and the Concourse was in Siberia.

"You got any details on that?" Piccolo said.

"Yes, let's see," Diaz said. "The driver's name is Earle Davis. From Gary, Indiana. Drove a Mack."

"What the fuck was he doing there?" Piccolo said. "That's a pretty wild area."

Diaz referred to the file.

"He said he was hauling a load of macaroni over to a warehouse on Arthur Avenue, and stopped to get a cup of coffee and a donut."

Frankenstein looked at one another. That was where Stein had been raised.

And it did make sense. The Arthur Avenue neighborhood was still unsullied by "progress." Indeed, the streets of Arthur Avenue were the same way they had been fifty years ago—clean, safe, and with a population that was almost exclusively Italian.

There was a reason. Members of Cosa Nostra lived in the neighborhood, and when the blacks had tried to

51

block bust they quickly had taken their show elsewhere after a number of them showed up in basements or lots just on the perimeter of the Arthur Avenue neighborhood, brutally knifed and with their genitals cut off, their bodies discarded like so much garbage.

A message had been sent.

Frankenstein spoke a few more minutes with Diaz and determined that the trucks and cars stolen were not all the same makes, though there were repeats—such as two Jags stolen—probably because the cars were profitable. But all the vehicles stolen shared one characteristic: they were new models.

Driving back to the station, Piccolo said, "Let's speak to Lawless."

"Yeah," Stein said, "there's more here than we thought."

"Absolutely."

CHAPTER 17

Piccolo and Stein were back at their apartment late in the day when Joe Lawless called them; they had left a message on his answering machine. Frankenstein could have beeped him, but both men were aware that he was involved with some nut-case bombing abortion clinics, and this wasn't really important enough to pull him away from that.

"Frank, how you doing? What have you got?"

Piccolo told Lawless how his nephew had his eighteen-wheeler stolen, and then about how the subsequent investigation had turned up a truck stolen within Siberia.

"I remember that," Lawless said. " Joyner took that

squeal. But he put it in the drawer. There weren't any leads at all."

"Right," Piccolo said.

"Do you want to take it, Frank?"

"Yeah, but first I'd clear it with Joyner. Tell him it was my nephew and all."

"Well, you have a lot on your plate," Lawless said, referring to the violent squeals Frankenstein was constantly dealing with.

"Yeah, I know. I can keep up with it—and this may be a big deal."

"I know. I'm just covering our behinds. I don't want to give Bledsoe any cause for getting on us. He'll ask why we're taking a flyer at a case like this when no one else has cleared it so far—rather than dealing with the homicides, etc. In other words what I'm saying is that you know he'll go for the numbers rather than the quality."

"Fuckin' A."

"Do it," Lawless said, as Piccolo knew he would. That was the way Lawless was. His squad was everything, and Piccolo well knew that he had often violated the book to back his men. Like Piccolo—Lawless had lied for him twice on brutality charges. Lawless's philosophy was that to get the job done you needed good people who got involved—and occasionally overexcited. He would put himself on the line for them.

"Thanks Joe," Piccolo said.

"Keep in touch."

Piccolo turned to Stein.

"You heard. But we still got to work on the other stuff."

"No problem," Stein said, and then reflected. "We could use a collar like this. Bring a chop ring down or something. Put that in our folders, make us real hard to fire."

"Fuckin' A," Piccolo said. " I don't think it would

mean bubkes to our so-called 'careers.' But it would be nice to shove it up the brass's ass. That's always a nice feeling."

"Believe it," Stein said.

CHAPTER 18

Frankenstein left their apartment four hours after they had spoken with Lawless, for a simple reason: the people who would most likely help them didn't work in the daytime. They were night people, hustling this, that, or the other thing, and their days began when most folks went to sleep. These were the people who could tell you the habits of alley cats, and what garbage cans and milk bottles sounded like in the early morning; they were people who had seen a thousand glorious dawns.

They were the snitches, the rats, the pigeons, the canaries, on whom detectives depended—despite the doggerel of TV and books—to clear most of their cases. They were the people who knew where the bodies were buried—and who buried them.

Frankenstein had discussed it and decided that they were the best way to go. For one thing, Suffolk had been probing this for a while, and had not come up with anything yet. For another, Frankenstein would bet that some canary somewhere knew something. Information on illegal activities was their stock in trade.

Frankenstein had five snitches—Piccolo three and Stein two. Piccolo had had five, and Stein three, but three were gone—dead. One of Piccolo's snitches had gotten heavily into crack and tried to rip off the wrong Jamaican. He had been jointed and interred without ceremony in four or five dumpsters in south Queens—no one knew for sure the number of dumpsters.

Another guy of Piccolo's and the other rat of Stein's had been caught plying their trades. Both had been clipped. Piccolo's guy was rumored to have been fitted for a concrete kimono and asked to take a leisurely stroll along the bottom of the East River. Stein's snitch had simply been shot in the head in his room, and his tongue removed with no regard for *Gray's Anatomy*.

Piccolo and Stein valued their snitches greatly, and both had tried hard to even the score for them. The guys who clipped the snitches did so, usually, because they were pissed and as an object lesson.

Piccolo and Stein wanted to nail the perps because it also sent a message: don't fuck with friends of Frankenstein. But in these instances they were not able to solve anything.

From their snitches, Frankenstein only asked two things: never lie and don't do certain crimes. Both Piccolo and Stein knew that their snitches were involved in crimes like burglary, fencing, gambling, using, stealing this, that, and the other thing, and both men looked the other way. It not only allowed the snitches to survive, but also gave them credibility among the people they were betraying. It worked out fine.

But the snitches knew the rules: If they were caught committing murder, assault with a deadly weapon, kidnapping, selling dope, or various other bad crimes, Frankenstein would withdraw their protection—and it would be bye-bye.

The prospect of going up the river had made more than one snitch whack himself. It was terrifying, because despite all their caution, certain people had a way of finding out who the rats were, and the punishment was easy to carry out in prison.

Stein had been able to reach one of his stoolies, a woman named Rita Bolanger, a midforties ex-hooker who was basically a small-time fence. She kept herself in good shape and would occasionally turn a trick for a quick fifty, and she had a knack for hearing things.

Rita was in a bar in Manhattan, one of three she

worked. Stein arranged to pick her up on Forty-fifth and Vanderbilt at two A.M. He told her he would have someone with him, but not to worry.

Piccolo had been unable to locate two of his snitches, but the one he did find was the best: August "the Ferret" Rondolpho.

Piccolo explained his attributes to Stein.

"This fucker could find out the last time the pope had diarrhea. He's smart, he's got big stones. He almost made into the Gotti family. I don't think anyone's ever suspected him. He's done a couple of bits, one in Attica, the other Dannemora, and he's never had a problem. He's told me I'm the only guy in the world knows he goes both ways. Now there's you, but I better meet him alone."

"How come he works for you?"

"I let him walk on a second-degree manslaughter. Got into a beef with a piece of shit named Winston Strachen, one of those real scumfuckers who will deal to their mothers if they have the bread. After that, he would probably let me butt-fuck him while he's telling me who's going down with what when."

"Sounds good."

"Tomorrow we'll see if we can track down the others. They're pretty good, too."

"So are mine."

CHAPTER 19

The man named Leo Molinari sat at the kitchen table. The woman named Sharon sat opposite him.

Sharon was scared. She knew Leo. When Leo hit this kind of mood, he could be very dangerous.

She had seen the mood coming all day. Usually Leo

was talkative. He should have been particularly talkative now, because he was doing real well in the theater. He had recently landed a part in a long-running off-Broadway show, and chances were he would be with it a long time.

And with Sharon's pay as a sales clerk at Fotomat, they would be doing okay, something that had not always been the case. There had been a time when Con Ed had turned off the lights. It had been bad.

But now it was not bad, and the silences began.

Leo would say nothing unless spoken to.

He would spend the day watching TV, or listening to the radio. A couple of times he went for walks.

And then, once, she had found him in the bedroom, in the dark, crying. She knew he was getting close to doing something.

She loved Leo, and she didn't want him to do bad things. Someday he was going to kill somebody, and then she wondered what she would do. What would she do without him?

It was a thought too horrible to bear.

"Leo," she said, "are you all right, honey?"

Leo's supper, a strip of fish, boiled potatoes, and spinach, was on a plate in front of him. He had not touched the meal.

"They're not listening to me," he said. "It's been a week since I told them to stop, and they have not stopped. Maybe they don't think I'll do anything."

"I don't think they think that," Sharon said. "I think they fear you. I do. You're not going to do anything, are you Leo?"

Tears had formed in Sharon's eyes.

Leo looked across the table at her. He felt like a cigarette, but he had none because he had quit smoking a year ago, as well as drinking, which he used to do a lot of. He put no impurities in his body. His body was a vessel for Jesus, and Jesus sometimes spoke to him.

In fact, he always wore an undergarment that reminded him and all who knew him of his priorities. It was a yellow T-shirt. On the front and the back was the legend, in three-inch-high black letters: JESUS IS LORD.

"You know what your problem is, Sharon?" Leo said.

She looked up at him. She had dark eyes. She blinked and a single tear ran down her cheek. Her mascara was smudged.

"You," he said, "don't have enough faith in Jesus, our Lord God. Nothing will happen to me, because God will protect me. And God will protect you, Sharon, if only you can take it in your heart to believe."

Another tear ran down Sharon's face, and she wiped it away.

Sharon wanted very much to believe, and she did believe, but not like Leo. Her faith could not be as strong as Leo's, because she wondered how God could take care of her.

"I'm trying to have faith, Leo. I've always believed in you."

"I know. But your faith must be deep and wide. Remember what Jesus said about faith: faith can move mountains."

Sharon nodded. She so wanted to please him. She had never met anyone like him. He was so handsome, so self-confident. He had such promise.

And then the thing with abortion started to interest him—and gradually possess him.

Sharon had gone along with him. She had no choice.

Sharon got up from the table and went over to him. She leaned down and kissed him on the cheek. He stiffened. He always stiffened when she kissed him. He was not comfortable with affection, even though he was very loving.

She stood looking down at him.

"You're not going to do something dangerous to-night, are you?"

He looked up at her, his large, dark eyes glittering. His eyes were so strange. Sometimes they were so alive and had such a twinkle in them. Yet sometimes something was missing: a focus, a certain connectedness with what was going on around him.

"Only," he said, "the work of the Lord."

Sharon went back to her seat and said nothing more. She didn't really want to know.

Sharon went to bed at around midnight, but she did not fall asleep until around one A.M.

Leo had gone in a little after her, and when he got under the covers she told him that she wanted to make love.

Leo was past the point of crying. Now he was excited by the prospect of what he was about to do, and it made him feel very erotic.

By two A.M. they made love three times, and Leo felt he could have gone on. But he had worn Sharon out, and by two-thirty he could hear her deep breathing. She was asleep.

He waited another ten minutes before he got quietly out of bed. He carried his clothes out of their small bedroom, then down a short hall into the bathroom. He closed the door and slowly got dressed. He didn't figure Sharon would get up. If she did she would think he had simply gone to the bathroom.

A few minutes later, dressed, he left the house, carefully and quietly closing the entry door behind him.

It was very cold out, which was good. When it was cold there were fewer people—fewer cops—on the street. People tended to stay inside. Everything slowed down.

Except the work of the Lord.

The dynamite was in a corner of the shed wrapped in black plastic. There was an entire case of it; he only needed a couple of sticks, but for just a moment he considered taking three.

Back in the house, he made the bomb on the kitchen table, first making sure that all the blinds were pulled.

He wore rubber gloves. He did not want to leave any prints on any of the components.

It was a simple affair. The two sticks of dynamite were secured with black tape to a small clock and a blasting cap.

He set the time for four A.M.

Then he inserted the fully assembled bomb into a plastic freezer bag and wrapped it in Saran Wrap. It was absolutely water tight.

He left the house.

Sharon owned a battered blue and white VW van, but he did not want to take a chance of it being spotted, or stopped by some cop. A search of the car would reveal the bomb.

No, it was better to go by subway. No one would stop him.

So he did that, and as he waited on the empty station platform at Vernon–Jackson for the train that would take him to Manhattan and then to the Bronx, he was aware that he might be in danger now because of the kinds of people who were out in the street. He knew the neighborhood where he was going was one of the worst in the city.

But he had no fear at all. What he had told Sharon was true. He was doing the work of the Lord, and the Lord Jesus would protect him. His body thrummed with the beauty and sadness, the joyfulness and rage of his mission.

CHAPTER 20

The guard at the J & L Clinic was named Joe Ruiz. Showcase, the name of the company he worked for, had been guarding the clinic around the clock since the bombing.

At first, Joe was on days, and that was much better than nights. During the day you got to see some fine-looking gash coming in the place, and Joe had made gentle passes at a couple of them, without success. Joe figured if they came to the clinic for an abortion they were pretty easy.

Nights were a different story.

Joe stationed himself, as Captain Reardon had told him, in the waiting room of the clinic. There were no windows to the outside, but the captain didn't want Joe listening to TV or the radio. He wanted him listening for any unusual sounds.

So all Joe did was sit in a chair, listening to the steam coming up, an occasional gurgle of a pipe, and the static from his walkie-talkie.

He should be able to have TV or radio. It was stupid not to have one. There was no way anyone could get into the place.

There was only one door, the front one, and the thing could resist King Kong.

The building was made of blocks, and was flanked by other stores with block walls. No way anyone could get in that way.

The back of the store, also block, butted against a brick apartment building. No way anyone could get in there without heavy equipment.

So that left the roof.

Like the other buildings on the block, this was a one-story job, with no skylight.

There was no way the guy could get in.

Joe figured this was just another case of Colonel Keefe, the big honcho at Showcase, wanting to make a big deal out of things so he'd be a big deal.

The building was long, and had lots of little rooms and doctors offices off a long hall. Down at the end was the operating room.

A couple of times since his assignment had started Joe had checked the rooms—not to see if a mad bomber was in there, but to check through drawers to see if he could find any pictures of naked women.

He didn't find any. What he found were medical pictures of pussies and insides and babies that made him want to puke. And he didn't like the smell of the place. Smelled like a morgue he had once guarded.

But a couple of times during the week he lay down on one of the examining tables, put his legs up in the stirrups, imagined some nice gash, and whacked off.

But after the second time he didn't do that because he had fallen asleep—with his pants down. Nothing like Keefe or Reardon coming in and seeing him up on an examining table with his uniform pants pulled down to his knees, his legs in stirrups.

At around 3:30, Joe Ruiz was sitting in the receptionist's chair, reading and half nodding off. He was not worried about a thing.

It was a two block walk from the subway to the J & L Clinic, and by the time Leo got to Tremont, about fifty yards away from it, his skin was red and taut and had lost some feeling.

Not that he noticed it. God was inside him now, and he was focused on looking for cops. After his notes to the mayor, someone could well be watching.

And there was always the possibility that a trap had been set.

Leo knew the clinics knew. Earlier in the week he had gone by three of them and noted that there were guards there. They would try to stop him.

He walked down Tremont, across the street from J & L, or the butcher shop, as he thought of it. He was separated by a spike-fenced underpass that routed traffic along Tremont, then under the Grand Concourse. The fence was good cover.

He glanced over, trying not to be obvious in case someone was watching. There were a number of apartment buildings on his side of the street where someone could spy. On the other side were one-story retail buildings, all closed.

He couldn't see anything dangerous.

He walked east along Tremont, which gradually dipped. He tried to act like a man just walking home on a wintry night.

The underpass ended at Anthony Avenue; he crossed Tremont, heading north. He was now about seventy-five yards from the clinic.

Anyone who had been watching him suspiciously wouldn't be now. He was walking *away* from the clinic.

But it also occurred to him that no matter what he did he was going to be exposed to danger. That was the way it was.

But he was willing to take the risk, for God and the still-unborn babies that he could save. His eyes teared.

God had commanded: stop them.

He would.

He continued up Anthony.

Some of the buildings on Anthony were abandoned; that was perfect for his purpose. But some were not abandoned. He would have to enter an occupied one.

He entered one about three-quarters of the way up the block. He knew that it backed on a laundromat only six stores away from the clinic.

The building was occupied, but the only sound he could hear was from a TV somewhere on an upper floor.

He climbed the marbleized stairs silently.

When he got to the first-floor landing he paused and opened a window a few inches. He got down on his haunches and peered out. It looked out on the store rooftops right below.

He could see no one. Across the street someone could be watching from any of the darkened windows, but there was no way for him to tell.

Jesus would keep him well, Jesus would protect him.

His eyes teared. He thought of the twenty-week-old fetus that an anti-abortionist preacher in the South had given him. It was all wrinkly and white, stuffed into a big jar filled with embalming fluid.

It had made him so angry when he saw it he threw up; he could not sleep for days. It opened up a door to a white-hot rage that could not be put out.

Jesus save me and all the little ones.

He opened the window. It squeaked and creaked, but there was nothing he could do.

He realized he was sweating.

As silently as he could, he dropped down onto the gravelly tar roof. He turned and closed the window in case someone would come down the stairs and be tempted to look out.

He was alone there now, alone on the roof with Jesus and the spirit of the little ones dead and gone.

Somebody had been on the roofs. There were a few old beer cans strewn about. It was the way the people of the city sunned themselves: Tar Beach, they called it.

They drank and sunned themselves while in air-conditioned rooms babies died.

Bastards!

He took the bomb from the sling under his coat and held it to his ear. Through the plastic he could hear dulled ticking.

From his jacket pocket he took a penlight and, shielding its glare, shone it against the bomb where the face of the clock was. The clock read 3:35. It was working perfectly.

He walked along the roofs, his shoes slightly crunching the gravel, until he was on top of the clinic roof. He knew there was a guard inside. He had to make as little noise as possible.

He went over to the sewer stack, a piece of pipe around three inches in diameter—commonly called a "stink pipe" by plumbers—jutted up around two feet.

He took the bomb out and uncoiled the cord secured to it. He inserted the bomb in the sewer stack—it fit easily—and carefully fed it down with both hands.

Though he had never seen the one in the J & L Clinic, he knew how sewer stacks were constructed. One of his many jobs before he was able to get fairly steady acting work was as a plumber's helper.

He figured he should go twelve feet. There was an eight-foot-high ceiling, and four feet between roof and ceiling. That would leave the bomb hanging inside the stack at about the level of the toilet.

The stack was cast-iron. When the dynamite detonated it would turn the stack into a grenade. Anyone who happened to be close by would get killed. That was not something he or God could be concerned with. If you lay down with butchers, you got butchered.

When he had played out twelve feet of line, he tied the end of the rope securely to the stack so it could not possibly slip and drop the bomb too deep into the system to do major damage to the clinic.

There was, actually, more than one stink pipe. There was one for each bathroom—a total of three. When he had first contemplated bombing the clinic, he had thought about doing all three, but he was not ready for that yet.

He would see what effect this one had.

With the bomb in place, securely tied, he went back across the roofs to the window. He pushed up the window, glanced left and right, and climbed through. He pulled it closed behind him, and fifteen seconds later was on the street.

He didn't realize how heavily he was sweating until the cold air hit his face. He felt good, very good.

Glory to God in the highest.

CHAPTER 21

The doctor who examined the guard, Joe Ruiz, in the ICU later said that he was lucky. He could easily have lost his life. At the moment the bomb detonated—precisely four o'clock—Joe Ruiz was heading for the bathroom to take a leak. Another few seconds and he would have been inside the bathroom.

That's why the doctor said he was lucky.

But Joe Ruiz didn't think of himself as lucky. He was twenty-two, and the bomb left him without his right eye and his left leg from the knee down.

His mother, Margarita, felt so bad for Joe, particularly one day when she was visiting him and he started to cry . . . from the only eye that was left. It was the saddest thing in the world.

The street, which had been deserted before the bomb went off, turned into a circus within five minutes after the occurrence. There were squad cars, EMS vehicles, a bomb truck, detective cars—seemingly a hundred revolving red lights. Watching from the sidelines were a couple of white-haired gents with Irish-looking faces that said brass, and a couple of candidates for political office in the city; there was nothing like someone else's pain and disaster to bring out the ghouls and political opportunists.

Of course the media were there, too, collectively salivating.

One female reporter for Channel Seven was heard lamenting that the injured guard didn't have a family, the implication being that nothing played on the early evening news like a broken-hearted wife and two or three confused and scared kids.

But they did shoot some footage of Ruiz's mother, asking her what she thought of her son's injuries.

Lawless and Freddie Billericks were also on the scene; Billericks had called in a couple of ATF agents to help sift the scene for evidence.

Happily for them, the first cop there had been a guy named Whalen, an old hairbag with twenty-nine years on the job who knew how to secure a crime scene. By the time Lawless and Billericks showed up, no one lower than the rank of captain could get in.

Lawless and Billericks looked over the devastation in silence for a while. Basically, the bathroom no longer existed, and neither did the wall to the hall or much of the ceiling in the front of the place. It was a wonder, Billericks noted, that there was no fire. That easily could have occurred, and Ruiz, who mercifully had been blasted into unconsciousness and remained that way until the day after he was operated on, would have burned to death.

But there was still the potential for a fire—and another explosion—when Billericks arrived. The sewer pipe had been shattered, sprayed like a grenade, so the sewer gases, including the explosive gas methane, were seeping into the area. It was not yet critical when Billericks arrived, but it could have gotten that way. He had the stack plugged with wet rags until repairs could be made.

Billericks quickly surmised something else. "This is no amateur, Joe. This guy knows how to handle his explosives."

It took Billericks and Lawless only a little while to figure out what had happened, because the front door was still bolted and heavily locked, and the pattern of the explosion was from the inside of the stack out.

The perp had somehow dropped the charge down the stack.

It was only when Billericks and Lawless got up on the roof, which they had lit up like day with strobe lights, that they understood exactly how it had been done.

The ATF guys took the rope that had been tied around the pipe and dusted the stack for prints. Neither Lawless or Billericks had much hope that they'd find anything.

They found some gravel on the windowsill and saw that the roof leading to the stack was disturbed slightly.

The window and sill were also dusted; even the doorknobs on the apartment building were done on the off chance that the perp had touched them before he put on gloves—assuming that he wore gloves.

As they watched the forensic people work on the roof, Billericks said, "Yeah, he's a pro—and clever. This is very hard to defend against."

Lawless nodded. Billericks didn't have to tell him that.

As the investigation proceeded, most of the crowd disappeared. The temperature was around twenty degrees, but a wind had started up and the vaunted "wind-chill factor" came into play.

But Leo, standing in the crowd behind crime-scene tape, did not leave.

He enjoyed what he saw, and one thought kept repeating itself to him: maybe now they would understand that he meant business. Maybe now they would stop killing.

CHAPTER 22

The next day Mike McAnne, the columnist for the *Daily News*, got a note from M.

Dear Mike,
I've been warning people about these butcher shops in the Bronx. They wouldn't listen so I've set two bombs off in one of them.
    You better tell them to listen or it will be very bad.
                    M, God's helper

McAnne made some calls and was fully filled in about the bombings of the J & L Clinic.

The *News* ran the note on page one; McAnne wrote a rehash of the activities of M, and speculated where it would end. There was no way, he said, that people were going to stop abortions, and it was his sense that there was no way M was going to stop retribution.

The column created a firestorm in City Hall and in the "Ivory Tower," as cops call One Police Plaza, NYPD headquarters. Just a few hours after the newspaper came out, the police commissioner, Crawford, badly pissed and upset, was on his way back from his vacation in Majorca with his wife.

Shortly after his plane touched down at Kennedy, Crawford and the mayor had a joint press conference to announce the formation of a special force to track the bomber.

Of course it was all blowing smoke. Crawford knew that the Five Three had some of the biggest fuckups ever to be in any police department anywhere, but he also knew that Joe Lawless was not among them. Crawford knew Lawless, and he had faith that he—coupled with the ATF—was going to do as good a job as he could expect.

All he and the mayor could hope was that they would come up with something quickly to get what Crawford called the "hyena press" off his back.

But the investigation was moving slowly.

An examination of the latents taken from the stack, windowsill, and elsewhere proved inconclusive.

The rope was a common nylon type widely available in hardware stores.

The dynamite used was standard, though it wasn't sold over the counter. You had to be licensed to get it, and every single stick had markings on it indicating place of origin: the city where it was manufactured, the factory, even the date and labor shift it was manufactured by. It could be traced precisely. But so far not enough remains of the sticks had been found to piece together the information.

A computer search by the ATF for known bombers and anyone who had been known to make a threat on abortion clinics had thus far proved fruitless.

One positive thing was that Ivette Gonzalez, the receptionist who had seen M at the J & L abortion clinic, had been able to remember enough detail on the man so that they had a composite drawing.

He appeared to be an average-looking man with rather heavy features, black hair, dark eyes, and a mustache. He wore glasses. Lawless would not bet on the man continuing to wear the glasses and mustache.

The police also canvassed the area to determine if anyone had seen anything, and thus far had come up negative. At that hour there were only a few people awake in the building the perp had entered to gain access to the roof, and they did not hear anything. Nor did anyone who lived in the building across the street notice anything.

One thing Billericks and Lawless saw: in addition to

being a fanatic, the guy they were looking for took chances. For quite a long time while he was on the roof he was directly exposed to view to anyone who happened to look out the window from across the street.

Yes, they were dealing with a dangerous man.

The *Daily News* columnist followed with another piece on the abortion bombings just two days after the first. Its theme was the small people who are seriously hurt when they are inadvertently drawn into the "arena where momentous events are being fought," and in this case the name of the innocent bystander was the guard, Joe Ruiz, who would forever bear the wounds of the battle because he just happened to be in the wrong place at the wrong time.

The *News* was giving *agita to* the PC and the mayor.

And to Bledsoe. Joe Lawless was constantly being bombarded with calls from Bledsoe, trying to find out what progress was being made on the case. A case like this was a Bledsoe nightmare: it invited scrutiny and criticism of higher-ups and, as such, threatened his position. He did not like that at all.

Lawless's answer was simple: "Nothing yet. I'll contact you when we get something."

Another detective might have been bothered by his CO constantly calling, but Lawless wasn't. He was a member of a police force, and ultimately he answered to superiors, but first and foremost he answered to himself. On any case he would always go one hundred percent, so no one could harass him for results. He knew he was doing the best he could, and that, to him, made him unassailable.

Forty-eight hours after the bombing the ATF lab in Washington, where the remnants of the bomb had been shipped, came up with something.

They had been able to piece together the paper covering on one of the sticks and get the information. The stick had been manufactured six months earlier by Renco Products in Joplin, Missouri.

Two hours after getting the information, Lawless and Billericks were on their way to Joplin to find out what they could find out. They had a lead.

CHAPTER 23

Kings Park Psychiatric Hospital was on the edge of Kings Park, a flat, less-than-beautiful town on the North Shore of Long Island that looked like it belonged on the South Shore, where towns were generally not nearly as good looking.

Two weeks after she had gotten involved in the rape case, Barbara Babalino drove out there from the city to visit with one of the victims—the first—a woman named Joan Keenan, who had been confined to the hospital since the attack on her and her fiancé, someone named George Gilbert.

Barbara had little hope that she would learn anything from Keenan. While the doctor at the hospital said she could communicate, he also said that she had suffered a deep trauma: the violation to her body had "seared her mind very badly."

Barbara also understood, though the doctor didn't go into details, that Gilbert, who had also been violated, was no longer her fiancé, and that he wouldn't talk with Barbara about what had happened the night they were raped.

Barbara didn't exactly understand the psychology of a person acting like that, but she sensed that it was similar to a man who would no longer be sexually interested in a wife or girlfriend who had been raped or had a mastectomy. In this case, the man's shame at his own violation could have made him more sympathetic to the woman's suffering. But it hadn't worked that way.

Barbara had already spoken to the female victim of the second couple, a woman named Anne Freda.

Anne Freda was a gutsy little girl.

She had recounted, in painstaking detail, what had happened. Several times she had started to cry during the telling, and once Barbara thought she was going to get ill.

Barbara maintained her composure as Freda told the story, but she found herself getting madder and madder.

In her police work—much to the chagrin of a number of fellow cops—Barbara could be concerned with the bad guy's background, where he came from, why he did what he did. But sometimes the crimes were so bad that she didn't think of that. All she thought about was revenge. This was one of those times.

The story, as it turned out, was heavy on horrendous detail, but short on usable fact for her investigation.

The couple had been out to dinner at a place called Amato's in Huntington, then had gone out for a few drinks and dancing at another place called Zuz.

They had gone home at about one A.M. Home was on Oakwood Road off Pulaski Road in Huntington. They had pulled their car behind the house and walked around to the front and gone inside.

"There's no rear entrance?"

"No," Freda said, "just the front."

"And you first became aware of this guy where?"

"Just as soon as we were inside the door. He came in after us."

"I see," Barbara said. She reflected on the assault in the Bronx. It felt like the rapist knew what he was getting into.

The conclusion that Barbara came to was simple: these people were not picked at random. They were selected, and then stalked.

73

Why they were picked, other than their attractiveness—all the couples were young and good looking—was another story.

Kings Park Psychiatric Hospital was immense, consisting of miles of lawn, now brownish in the winter, and clusters of massive faded redbrick buildings, many of them with barred windows.

The approach to the Administration Building was a long asphalt road flanked by trees that were gnarled and twisted, as if symbolic of the mental state of most of the inhabitants of the place.

Barbara had had occasion to visit a number of mental hospitals during her life, both on a professional basis and when her now-deceased ex-husband had been committed as a result of drug use. She had never gotten used to it.

Barbara was taken to see Joan Keenan by a Dr. Marks, who said as they walked down a hall toward the visitors room, "She may not be able to answer your questions. She's medicated rather severely. She was a fragile personality to start with, and these events had a searing impact."

Barbara waited for Joan Keenan in the regular visiting room of the hospital, which consisted of a number of Formica tables, some plastic-covered chairs, a couple of tables, and about fourteen ashtrays. As a group, mental patients smoked like a collective chimney.

Something squeezed Barbara's insides when Joan Kennan came into the room.

Barbara knew she was twenty-two, but she already had that droopy mental-ward look. She had dark hair, that had not been combed, no makeup, and there were dark rings under her eyes.

She wore a loose, nondescript dress. She looked defeated, her eyes barely alive.

Dr. Marks introduced Barbara and then left.

As gently as she could, Barbara told Joan Keenan why she was there, to see if she could find out additional details on the assault.

Joan Keenan looked at her blankly, her brow slightly fretful.

"What assault?" she said.

"Oh," Barbara said, "there was an assault that you were involved in. Do you remember that?"

She looked at Joan. The woman shook her head.

"I don't remember anything like that."

Barbara nodded. Jesus, she thought.

"Do you know anyone named George Gilbert?" Barbara asked.

A quick smile wreathed Joan Keenan's face.

"Of course I do," she said, "that's my fiancé."

Barbara hesitated a moment, then said. "How often do you see him?"

"He used to visit every day."

"Used to?"

"Well, he can't now. He's away."

"Where is he?"

"He went across the sea. Far away."

"Do you know when he's coming back?"

A dark cloud passed across Joan Keenan's face.

"Not for a while. A long while."

Barbara felt a little thickening in her throat.

"I'm sorry to hear that."

"Thank you." Joan Keenan said. Her eyes had misted. She was breaking Barbara's heart, but Barbara had to continue.

"Before you saw him every day, where did you see him?"

"Before here?"

"Yes."

"At his house or mine. He used to come over. Or I'd go over his house."

"Where do you live?"

"768 Palmer Road, Northport."

"And him?"

"Same place. Lives with me."

"I see," Barbara said. She had a different address for Gilbert.

"How long have you lived together?"

"Six months."

"I see. Do you like it?"

"Its okay. Pallone isn't the best."

"Who?"

"Pallone. The landlord. Not the best. Doesn't do all he should do. We have a leak in the roof."

"I see," Barbara said. "But you're happy with George."

"Happiest I've ever been in my life."

Barbara looked at Joan Keenan. Her mind was walled off from what happened that night. It was as if her memory had stopped functioning just before the assault.

This sometimes happened to people who suffered a trauma. Most of the time they came back. Sometimes they didn't.

Barbara's instincts told her that Joan Keenan would not come back, that she would be locked out of her life forever because she could not go past that night.

Barbara thought she would try one other approach.

"Did you hear," she asked, "about that couple who lived near you who were assaulted?"

Joan Keenan had light blue eyes. For a moment Barbara saw a blink of recognition, then a narrowing. It scared her. She could not even get close to it that way.

"No," she said, "I didn't hear anything like that."

Barbara looked at her for a moment. Then she reached across the table and touched her hand.

"Thanks for your help," she said. "You've been very helpful."

* * *

Fifteen minutes later, Barbara was driving up the long, tree-flanked asphalt road that led out of the facility.

Overall, she thought, she had gotten nothing significant so far from anyone, particularly Joan Keenan.

But she was wrong.

CHAPTER 24

Within a week after Frankenstein put the word out to their snitches, they had all but the Ferret's report in.

It was all negative, though one of Stein's snitches, Ronny Beason, said that he heard that "wiseguys was involved." That's all he had been able to come up with.

Stein gave him a fifty and told him to keep digging.

Piccolo met the Ferret at a bar in Westfield, New Jersey, which struck Piccolo as being a little too cautious. "We might as well meet in fucking Long Spear, Idaho," Piccolo had commented—but he did not want to pretend to tell the Ferret his business. The Ferret had taken part in some very big time stings involving some of the most vicious bad guys around, and the efficiency and skill with which he conducted business was attested to by the fact that he was, as he liked to say, "still ambulatory and taking nourishment."

The Ferret was a very odd looking human being. He had a long, prominent nose, dark, glossy black hair, small, dark protruding eyes, and he was very skinny.

And short—a couple of inches shorter than Piccolo, who was five-five. That was probably one reason why Piccolo liked the Ferret so much.

In a way, Piccolo and the Ferret looked alike. If human beings had evolved through a series of developments, becoming more and more refined as the models went along, then the Ferret was the last stage of development before Piccolo. He was Piccolo unfinished, without the details and the varnish.

But the Ferret was more educated than Piccolo. The Ferret had finished two years of a community college in Los Angeles, where he grew up, was a voracious reader, and had a gift for numbers.

Which is what led to the bit he had done in Sing Sing. He was involved in a big bank scam. He had used his natural abilities for ill-gotten gain.

He had also done one year in Dannemora for fencing.

The Ferret—he hated the nickname—had told Piccolo that he had loathed the years in prison.

"You've got every brand of psychopath found in the Abnormal Psych books—and some they haven't. People spend their days raping and killing each other when they're not playing stupid territorial games. An altogether loathsome experience."

So Piccolo could not understand why the Ferret was still into crime. Piccolo knew very well he was doing stuff that could put him back inside—if Piccolo wasn't there to protect him—but he kept doing it anyway.

The Ferret explained it once. "It's a compulsion I have," he said. "I like living on the edge. I have the philosophy of the circus Wallendas. After they all fell off the high wire down in Puerto Rico—one got killed and several were injured—some reporter asked the oldest Wallenda if they were going back up on the wire, and he said, 'Going back up? *Life is the wire. All else is waiting.*' That's me. Crime is my wire."

They met at around three o'clock in the afternoon. The bar was a typical neighborhood place. There was a single large room with a polished mahogany bar on one side and booths and tables scattered through the rest of the room. It smelled slightly of booze and disinfectant.

The place was empty except for a couple of older guys at the bar. A country-western song was playing on the jukebox.

78

Piccolo and the Ferret sat in one of the booths. A chunky waitress took their orders.

"So how you doing, August?" Piccolo asked. He never called the Ferret the Ferret.

"Still looking for Old Yeller," he said.

Piccolo knew he was referring to the one big deal he had said he was looking for all his life that would make him fiscally free. He picked it up from a song sung by the old actor Walter Brennan about a gold miner.

"When you find it," Piccolo said, smiling—he had his teeth in—"don't fucking tell me."

A slight smile played around the Ferret's lips.

"You know I wouldn't break the law."

"Yeah," Piccolo said, "and my grandmother's balls hang down to her knees."

The Ferret smiled.

The drinks, a seven and seven for Piccolo, a white wine for the Ferret, were brought to the table. The waitress left.

"So what have you got?" Piccolo said.

The Ferret's eyes darted from side to side, and he glanced around the bar. Piccolo knew that was a habit the Ferret had when he was nervous.

"The Capezzis," the Ferret said. "They're the ones behind this."

"Philadelphia?"

"That's right."

The Ferret was referring to the biggest, strongest Mafia family in Pennsylvania.

"What are they doing?"

"Everything," the Ferret said. "They operate mostly out of movie theater parking lots and take new cars as well as eighteen-wheelers. The eighteen-wheelers are an expanding part of their business."

The Ferret took a long sip of the wine. He grimaced.

"This tastes like vinegar."

"Want something else?"

"No."

There was a pause.

"So what do they do?" Piccolo asked.

"They chop some of them, but from what I understand there's a big market for big rigs in South America. They're making a mint."

"They're stealing from different states, right?"

"Jersey, New York, PA, Ohio, etc. They got a lot of people working for them."

"Any chance for an introduction?"

The Ferret took another a tiny sip of his wine. He shook his head.

"Too dangerous," he said. "You ever heard of Angelo Capezzi?"

"Yeah."

"He's grotesque looking—built like Jabba the Hutt—and as vicious as they come. But he's smart. Very hard to fool."

Piccolo said nothing.

The Ferret beckoned to the waitress. She came over and took his order for a bottle of Amstel Light. He pushed the wine to one side.

"Figure bottles come with caps on," the Ferret said. Piccolo ordered nothing.

"I heard," the Ferret went on, "that Capezzi fell in love—if that's what you want to call it—with another woman when he was about thirty. But he had three kids and a wife. So what did he do? They say he had his first wife clipped so he could marry his second in a church ceremony. A real good Catholic."

Piccolo looked at him. He said nothing.

"The other thing is twice they tried to sting him. But somehow he found out about the guys who went undercover and they disappeared. I mean he had cops whacked—get the message? Nobody will risk trying to go inside."

"What you're telling me is that you want limited involvement in this?"

The Ferret shook his head.

"No involvement."

"I think I could go in there myself and work some things."

"I'd be worried for you. And me. I mean, what kind of intelligence does Capezzi have that lets him find *two* undercovers? That's scary."

"Could you help me get in?"

The Ferret sipped the beer. His hand shook ever so slightly.

"Look Frank," he said, "I've given you three big busts, but I'm afraid of this."

Piccolo took a long sip of his drink. Then he reached into an inside pocket and pulled out a wad of cash.

He handed it to the Ferret.

"What's this?" the Ferret asked.

"Five hundred dollars. Down payment on the five large I'm going to pay you when you get me inside."

The Ferret stared at the money.

"That's right. And it's the usual deal. I will not ID you to anybody, except my new partner. And one other thing. After this is over I will not ask you to do anything fucking like it again. Ever."

"It's too dangerous," the Ferret said. He kept looking at the money.

"Where you going to get five large?"

"Don't worry about that. You'll get it. Once I'm in, you got it." They sipped their drinks in silence. Piccolo smiled.

"This will be your ultimate," Piccolo said, "the grand fucking finale of your life on the wire. High up, higher than you've ever been, and one misstep and you fall into a moat filled with fucking starving alligators from Ethiopia."

Piccolo smiled. He liked the imagery.

The Ferret picked up the money and slipped it into his pocket.

"You sure know how to finesse me, don't you Frank?"

CHAPTER 25

Four days after he met the Ferret, the Ferret arranged for Piccolo to meet with Vito Capezzi, a nephew of Angelo and a button man in the family.

They met in the back of Aldo's Pizzeria on Market Street in downtown Philadelphia. Seated in a booth were Piccolo, Vito Capezzi, and the Ferret.

Piccolo had considered wearing a wire, but then had decided against it. It might be risky at this point. He left his .44 Magnum home, but carried a Beretta in a jock holster.

Stein was also there. He had been working his way through a full Italian dinner, when the other three men showed up. He had three guns on him.

Plus his fist.

Vito Capezzi, Piccolo guessed, was near thirty and had punk written all over him. He wore tight black pants, a silver shirt open at the throat showing black chest hair and heavy gold, a black jacket, overcoat, and black shades. His hair was black and his fingers were decorated with four rings, two of them diamonds.

They ordered drinks—the Ferret wine, Piccolo a mixed drink, and Capezzi a small chilled bottle of San Pellegrino with wedges of lemon and lime.

They did not shake hands. Macho men never shook hands.

Capezzi spoke first.

"The Ferret here says you can supply us with some stuff."

The Ferret looked sharply at Capezzi but said nothing.

"Yeah, I can."

"What have you got?"

"What do you need?"

"I'll ask the questions."

"I'm just trying to get a line on your marketing needs."

"What, you got a factory to produce what we need?"

Piccolo shook his head and smiled. No scumfucker, he thought.

"Tell me what you got," Capezzi said.

"For starters a Jaguar."

Capezzi shrugged.

"How new is it?"

"This year."

"We don't take nothing from last year. This year's models only, got it?"

Piccolo nodded. He wondered what this guy would feel like if he whipped out the Beretta and shoved the barrel in his mouth. Stain his fucking pants.

There was a silence. They sipped their drinks.

Piccolo decided it was best to let Macho Man lead the parade.

Capezzi turned toward the Ferret and smiled a little. Piccolo could see himself and the Ferret reflected in the shades, which were rounded. He wondered how the motherfucker could see—the joint wasn't all that well lit.

"How long you guys know each other?" Capezzi said.

It was not idle conversation.

"Long enough, Mr. Capezzi," the Ferret said, his brow knitting. He wanted Capezzi to know he didn't like to be questioned about his friends. The Ferret vouched for them and that was enough.

On the other hand, he didn't want to show disrespect.

Capezzi sipped his drink. If he pursued it, the Ferret might have to take a stand, and possibly blow the deal— and five large.

Piccolo understood the game the Ferret was playing. If you let it all go down too easy, the wiseguys might get suspicious.

Capezzi said nothing more.

Piccolo spoke. "So are you interested in the Jag, Mr. Capezzi?" he said.

"Probably. I'll get back to you."

"Okay."

"When could you have it?"

"Whenever and wherever you say."

Capezzi nodded.

"Could you give me an idea how much you pay?"

"I'll get back to you," Capezzi said. And with that he got up and left the restaurant.

When he was well out of earshot, Piccolo said, "Think he'll get back to me?"

"Yeah," the Ferret said, and Piccolo noticed that fine beads of sweat had emerged on the Ferret's temples.

CHAPTER 26

The night of the day they talked to Capezzi, Frankenstein was back on the streets of Siberia, conducting their regular investigations. They told Lawless that they were making progress on the case, but kept it a little vague. He would not have approved of what they were doing.

That same night they got a call from the Ferret at the station.

He had a message from Vito Capezzi.

"We got the go ahead. He wants the Jag," the Ferret said, "within forty-eight hours."

"Where does he want it?"

"Philadelphia. You're to take it to Delaware Street and Hook Road and call a certain number when it's delivered. Somebody will pick it up right away."

"When do we get paid?"

"Vito said that he'll contact us on where to pick up the money after the car is delivered."

"How much?"

"Three thousand."

"Okay. We're going to get the car tonight. I'll call you when we're set to go."

CHAPTER 27

In terms of equipment, the New York City Police Department is schizophrenic. Most of the station houses are old and need repair to one degree or another. And the paperwork is done on some machines, such as brown manual Royal typewriters, that are ancient.

But for identification and other functions the department has a computer system that is state of the art.

One of the standard functions of the system is to tie in with the New York State Motor Vehicle Bureau, and using this feature it didn't take Frankenstein long to find out what they wanted.

They made a list of five cars, all brand new and owned by wiseguys: two Cadillacs, an Alfa Romeo, and two Jaguars.

One Jag was owned by Aldo Fischetti, *capo regime* of the Buscetti family. He had bought it four months earlier.

Fischetti lived in Waync, New Jersey, which was good. In fact, Frankenstein intentionally picked people who lived in the suburbs, where security on the cars was likely to be lighter. In the city people didn't keep their cars on the street without taking as many precautions as they could, and many of them had alarm systems.

Frankenstein quickly agreed that Fischetti was a good

first mark, and they loved the idea that someone would be stealing something from him for a change.

"That's neat," Piccolo said.

They decided to try the house first. If Fischetti parked the car on the street, or in the driveway, they could get it easy.

If not, they would have to track him a bit and pick it up wherever he left it.

They drove to Wayne in a huge Ryder van. They found Fischetti's house, then parked the van about five blocks away.

Then they walked around until about midnight and approached the Fischetti house on foot.

Piccolo carried a small overnight bag, in which there was the equipment for getting the car going. They figured that if they were stopped by cops—not a farfetched possibility—they would simply flash their tin and say they were on stakeout. Local cops knew the bad guys, so they would likely think Fischetti was the target.

But in that case Frankenstein would have to abandon Fischetti. Just to be on the safe side, they had another guy named Buleo, who lived in Freehold and who also had a Jaguar, as a backup.

They saw no one on their way to Fischetti's house. It was another cold night.

Most of the houses were set well back from the road, surrounded by big, rolling, fenced-in lawns.

The Fischetti house was not visible from the road; they knew that getting the car wasn't going to be simple if he didn't, by some miracle, leave it on the street.

They saw that he didn't.

There was a main entrance with big fancy gates, and a spiked wrought-iron fence about six feet high. The place had to be at least five acres.

They stood by the fence but away from the gate.

"I don't see no camera, Howie. Do you?"

"No, but there could be one."

Piccolo knew what he meant. The asphalt driveway,

86

which snaked up a long hill and had ground-level lights that made it look like a curving airport runway, was flanked by heavy trees. Most of the trees were bare, but those near the fence were evergreens, and it would be easy to mount a camera out of sight on any of the branches.

Other than the lights on top of the tall brick gateposts, there was no other dangerous illumination.

"I think we should go over the fence somewhere else," Piccolo said, "then we'll cut the lock on the gate before we go. That might be alarmed."

"He might have ultrasonic around the joint, too."

"Maybe, but we got to take that chance."

"Okay, Frank."

They walked back the way they had come until they were at a point some fifty yards away from the gate.

The fence was decorative rather than strictly for security; every twenty yards or so there was a large brick post into which the ends of the fence sections were mortared. They decided to go over one of these.

They glanced each way.

The street was quiet, dark except for a couple of houses a good distance down the block that had their lights on. The only thing moving was the steam coming out of a manhole far down the block.

Wordlessly, Piccolo went over to one of the posts and grabbed the sides of it.

Stein grabbed him around the waist and helped him up, until he could grab the top and pull himself over.

Piccolo dropped down behind the fence hidden by heavy trees.

Stein needed no help. He jumped slightly, his left hand grasping the top of the post, and pulled himself up about a foot, then grabbed with the other hand and pulled himself up all the way.

He dropped down into the yard.

There was no way to know if the fence was alarmed, and if they had just set it off, but they would find out soon enough.

They threaded their way quickly through the trees in the direction of the house, and gradually its lights came into view.

There were Par security lights mounted on each corner of the house, which was huge, white, fancy—definitely the work of an Italian architect. It was very well lit.

The house had two stories, and some lights on the second floor were lit. There was no other sign of life. It didn't seem like there were any ultrasonic devices in place, but Frankenstein did notice the slim metallic tape on the windows—they were alarmed.

The garage was on the other side of the house, but that was no big problem. They could travel the woods all the way.

When they got to the other side they saw a sight for sore eyes: the black Jaguar, glistening in the security lights, was parked in the driveway.

Frankenstein thought the same thing: leaving the car in the open like that must have meant he started it electronically, to protect against having his ass blown up; or maybe he felt that no one would mess with a high ranking fucker like him.

Whatever, the car was there.

Frankenstein had agreed on what their roles would be back at the station. Stein was to open the door with a Slim Jim—a thin metal bar that could be slipped between the door and glass to pull the latch on the lock up, so the door could be popped.

Piccolo was to be ready with the come-along—a device that would tear out the ignition so the car could be hot wired.

The car could be on its way down the driveway in a minute.

But then Piccolo had what he thought was a better idea.

"Look," he whispered, "you open the door, I'll get in, and release the brake and we'll let this fucker roll down the driveway, okay?"

"You got it."

They exited the cover of the woods.

Stein went first, followed by Piccolo. Piccolo felt like he had years ago when he ran naked through the girls bathroom on a dare in school.

They were focusing on the car, so they did not see the black blur that came around the side of the house.

The next few moments seemed to be in slow motion, but they happened at high speed.

The black blur was a pit bull terrier, and he was coming at them, his claws making the only sound, at about thirty miles an hour.

Piccolo went for his gun, but it was too late. The pit bull was airborne.

But it was not too late for Thunderfist.

Stein brought his arm around in a short, savage blur, and his fist collided with the pit bull's open, slavering jaws.

The jaw went crunch, and the pit bull fell toward the driveway, unconscious before it hit the asphalt, where it flopped like a hunk of dead meat.

Frankenstein did not pause for analysis. In a moment Stein had the car open and Piccolo was in it. Stein pushed, and the car started to roll silently down the driveway.

In a flash, Stein was in the passenger seat, and there was still no one in sight.

Piccolo negotiated the curved driveway to the end by the gate, stopped the car, and then did mayhem to the ignition with the come-along.

A moment later Stein, who had leaped out of the car even before it stopped, severed the gate lock with big bolt cutters. When he heard the car thrum to life he swung the gates open—and in the distance immediately heard the muted clanging of an alarm.

He was in the car, and they were down the block, around the corner, and five blocks away by the time the first button man, armed with an Uzi, was out of the house and saying, "What the fuck's going on?"

They pulled up behind the big truck they had come in, and Stein got out quickly. He pushed the back door up, and then pulled two ramps onto the street.

Thirty seconds later Piccolo had driven the Jaguar into the truck, and the back door was pulled down and locked.

Then Stein climbed into the driver's seat, Piccolo the passenger seat.

Stein fired up the truck and put it in gear. They were off.

"Christ," Piccolo said, "it's a good thing we became cops. We would have made some evil motherfuckers."

They guffawed in the darkness of the cab.

CHAPTER 28

Like most cops, Lawless had never been to a dynamite factory, but he was not surprised when he first saw it, from a half mile away, as he and Freddie Billericks approached it by car.

"All the dynamite factories are isolated," Billericks said. "This one's got about six hundred acres of free space around it. That's about three times more than the average missile silo."

"How often they go up?"

"Rarely. Even when they first started they were extremely safety conscious."

The building, made of block, didn't look much different from any other factory, except there seemed to be more plumbing on the outside.

They parked in an employee parking lot at the rear of the building, then went inside to find Roger Green, the manager of the plant.

The day before, Billericks had called him and told

him about the dynamite having the markings of that plant on it, and that he should check what he had in storage to see if anything was missing.

They were introduced to Green, who was an ordinary looking man—one might have suspected him to have the volatile personality of a heart surgeon. He occupied a glass-enclosed office on a catwalk that looked down onto the main manufacturing area.

They had to wait a few minutes while Green tied up some business, and Lawless spent the time observing the making of dynamite.

There was, he saw, a large canister in which the material was mixed. Beneath it, empty, kraft-covered tubes of paper rotated and were filled with the material, much as one might fill pastries with a pastry bag. There was some sort of device that tamped the dynamite into the tubes, and then they travelled down a conveyer belt to be packed by hand into boxes.

It all looked so ordinary, Lawless thought. The workers even looked bored.

But dynamite was incredibly powerful. Lawless recalled a bomb squad guy once telling him that a dynamite explosion exerted energy pressure at a speed of over 1700 feet a second—three miles a second. That was power.

"Will you come in please, gentlemen?" Green said.

Lawless and Billericks went inside and Green directed them to a couple of chairs in front of his desk, which was very neat.

He got right down to business, directing his comments to Billericks, whose agency, of course, had responsibility for the regulating of dynamite.

"We checked inventory," Green said, "and we did have a theft. A case."

"Sixty or a hundred and twenty sticks?" Billericks asked.

"A hundred and twenty."

"When?"

"We don't know precisely. We store the dynamite

for periods of two to three weeks before it is shipped. We know that it was stolen from six to eight weeks ago from magazine twelve."

"Signs of a break-in?"

"Yes," Green said. "Would you like to see it?"

"Yes," Billericks said.

They drove to the storage site in Green's car. As they went he explained, more for Lawless's edification than Billericks's, the procedure at Renco.

"We don't take any special precautions storing the dynamite, as you'll see. It's just stored in half-buried igloos and placarded—"

"What's that?" Lawless asked.

"Posted with DANGER signs," Green answered, then continued. "There's plenty of space around the igloos and a simple farm fence. We don't need more. It keeps the kids away, and people in the area simply don't bother it."

"And," Lawless said, "you said you don't know when the theft occurred."

"No, because once it's stored no one sees it again until it's shipped."

"I see."

They drove in silence to the magazine where the theft had occurred. Green showed them the pried door, and explained the construction of the storage facility—concrete block lined with four inches of hardwood—which was designed more to resist bullets than thieves.

To Lawless, it looked like the door had been pried open with some sort of metal bar.

Inside, cases of dynamite were stacked up.

"These," Green said, "are ready to be shipped. There's about fifty thousand pounds here."

There wasn't much to see, Lawless thought. At this stage the chance of getting prints was remote at best. And he recalled that the suspect who came into J & L wore gloves. Why would he not wear them here?

* * *

As they returned to Green's office, Green told them, at Billericks' request, that he would furnish them a list of the all the employees Renco had used over the last three years.

"Blasters among them?" Billericks asked. It was more likely for workers who were qualified as blasters to be suspects than those who weren't.

"Yes," Green said. "There were more than a few."

An hour later, Billericks and Lawless were in the car on their way back to New York City. One central fact was uppermost in each man's mind. A case of dynamite with 120 sticks was missing, and in the possession of a fanatic.

CHAPTER 29

Wrigley's had tracked the couple for a week and felt sure that he knew everything he needed to know.

He actually wanted to track them some more, but in doing that there was always the danger that he would be noticed.

Anyway, it was time for the kill. All his senses were alert and alive, and he felt the heavy fullness in his groin. It was time to unload himself into living bodies. Time to show his superior intelligence and power.

The couple was the biggest of the ones he had tracked. The man had to be at least six-three and the woman almost six feet.

And not skinny or puny. The man was built like a tight end in football, the woman like some other kind of athlete. They were like big trees, waiting to be taken down.

By him.

He liked that.

There was only one problem. The house they lived in, a private one in Northport, a town near Huntington, had two other tenants, and they always seemed to be around.

There was no way, Wrigley's figured, he could get them alone in the house without danger of being discovered.

He would have to do something else.

He thought about it for a day or so, then made a plan. It should all work very well, as long as Ketcham, the marked male, kept his cool. If he didn't there could be problems.

Wrigley's decided to do it on a Friday night, early. The couple had gone out the previous Friday night and done some drinking. Wrigley's didn't want to try to handle them when Ketcham had booze in him. That might be risky.

Sally Binns and Jake Ketcham did decide to go out Friday night. In fact, they usually went out at least one night of the weekend.

Both worked hard. Ketcham was an auto mechanic and Sally worked in the collection department at A&S. By the time the weekend came along, they were both a little stressed out. Both, in their way, were always dealing with the public in an adversarial role. That would stress anyone out.

When they got home Friday, though, they did not feel like going to a bar. Both had had particularly hard days.

Ketcham had gotten involved in an altercation with a customer on a transmission job while Sally had had to deal with some psycho who said that he was going to come down to A&S and break her legs.

A movie seemed more like both their speeds, and there was a new Chevy Chase movie playing at the Whitman, in the Walt Whitman shopping center.

They decided to eat out, then catch a ten o'clock show.

94

They left the house about eight o'clock, and drove to Harvey's Diner on Jericho Turnpike.

They made it a rule not to talk about business. No sense upsetting digestion.

They ate a leisurely dinner, and left the restaurant about 9:30. It was a ten-minute drive to the theater, but it would take them a little longer tonight because it was sleeting by the time they left the restaurant. They did not expect a crowd, particularly because the weather had turned bad.

They were right. There were relatively few cars in the parking lot that served the Whitman and a bank of stores. And there was no one, as far as they could see, on line except for two people standing at the glassed-in booth buying tickets.

Ketcham had stopped their van and was about to get out when he heard the noise.

He turned and at the same moment Sally screamed.

"Shut up," Wrigley's, who had his ski mask on, growled. "And don't get cute or I'll blow her brains out."

Wrigley's had a 9 mm automatic pressed against the back of her head—he would do it. He wondered what it would feel like to see someone's brains spatter all over the interior of a car. And on him.

Ketcham's eyes widened.

"Drive out of here," the man said, "and head south on 110."

Ketcham hesitated. Wrigley's was glad he was not drunk. He would have to watch him very carefully.

The van jerked at first, but then Ketcham got it running smoothly. Sally whimpered and sobbed as they drove. It was like a lamb bleating to a tiger.

They drove slowly down 110, a main, four lane artery running north and south on Long Island. And as they did Wrigley's saw a police car coming the other way. He tensed, watching it. He knew Ketcham saw it, too. He wondered if Ketcham was going to try something heroic.

If he did, he would die. Wrigley's knew that if he

was caught doing this he would be in prison the rest of his life.

Ketcham did nothing, and the police car faded into the distance behind them.

Just before they reached the entrance to the Northern State Parkway west, Wrigley's barked a command.

"Turn in here."

Ketcham hesitated a millisecond.

"Turn in!"

He turned in.

They were on a narrow dirt road that ran west adjacent to the parkway. The road continued that way for perhaps two hundred yards, then it turned into a dense, woodsy area, which opened out into a small open area.

"Stop!"

The van stopped.

"You, woman, get out."

Sally got out. Wrigley's got out with her, keeping one eye on her and one on Ketcham.

"Stop," he commanded. She stopped.

"Hands behind your back."

She put her hands behind her back. Quickly, expertly, he cuffed her with one free hand.

"Back in the van. In the back."

She got back in. He liked the curves of her body as she stepped up and in. It was all his.

"Out here, big man."

Ketcham got out. Wrigley's walked slowly toward him.

Wrigley's was undecided. Maybe he should have some fun with him. But he was a very big man. As skilled and tough as Wrigley's was, he might still have problems. He handled the first guy, Gilbert, but he was much smaller than this guy. He didn't know . . . .

Then Ketcham decided for him. When Wrigley's was within two feet of him he lunged for the gun.

Wrigley's was quick as a cat. He stepped back out of the way and brought the side of the pistol up against Ketcham's head with sickening force. The big man fell to his knees, dazed, and then Wrigley's kicked him in the head and again when he hit the ground.

"Oh please, no," Sally said from the van. "Please," she choked.

Wrigley's turned Ketcham over and used both hands to cuff him. The man was regaining consciousness when he dragged him into the van.

He pushed him roughly to the floor of the van, then pushed the girl down roughly next to him on her stomach.

He took a roll of duct tape from the floor and wrapped it roughly around each of their mouths.

He looked at them for as long as he could, then proceeded to strip their clothing off with a straight razor.

He quivered with power.

CHAPTER 30

Barbara heard about the assault within five hours of its happening.

Bickford called her.

"Wrigley's hit again," he said. "A white couple from Northport. A guy, twenty-four, and his girlfriend, twenty-three. The guy's in the hospital, the girl is all right."

"What's the matter with the guy?"

"Has a concussion. He got hit on the head."

"Where did it happen?"

Bickford gave her details. Barbara wondered why Wrigley's had broken his pattern. All the other assaults were indoors.

"They could have died," Bickford said. "When he was finished with them he threw them out of the van like so much dirty laundry—and they were both nude with the temperature around twenty. They were found by some kids who came into the area. As it was, they were close to frostbite."

"What hospital is the guy in?"

"Northside in Huntington."

"Can he talk?"

"Yes."

"Will he?"

"He said he would."

"How about the female?"

"Yes, her too."

"I hope they have something for us."

"They were trying to notice as much as they could about Wrigley's as he did his number. Maybe they will."

CHAPTER 31

It was another twenty-four hours before Barbara was able to see the couple who had been assaulted. She saw the man first. Doctors said that the woman, Sally, was not yet ready to talk.

Jake Ketcham was sitting by a window with his back to her when she came in; she almost winced when he turned.

His head was swollen. One eye was a slit, one side of his jaw was puffy, and that entire side of his head was discolored, red and purple.

When she saw him, she realized just how tough Wrigley's must be. Ketcham was a big man, and he seemed in excellent condition. Wrigley's would have to be very tough indeed.

"May I?" Barbara asked, motioning to a chair near him.

"Sure."

Barbara sat down.

"How's your girlfriend doing?" she asked, even though she knew.

"Okay, I guess. How could anybody do, right?"

Barbara nodded.

There was a short silence, then Barbara spoke again.

"I understand you have some details on the assailant."

"Yeah," Ketcham said. "I do."

He paused. Barbara could feel the anger like heat.

"I tried to notice stuff that I thought might be helpful."

He inhaled deeply, grimaced.

"He wore a mask," Ketcham said, "but at one point I was able to see his eyes. They were dark brown."

Barbara jotted the fact down in a small notebook she had taken out.

"He was dressed in dungarees and a black leather jacket. He wore black boots."

"Good," Barbara said.

"His hair was black. He wore black leather gloves, but there was part of one wrist showing and I saw black hairs."

Barbara nodded, jotting it down.

"The other thing," Ketcham said, "was his smell. I know the smell. He uses Polo after-shave."

"Good," Barbara said, "very good."

Ketcham took a deep breath. The details were not easy. They were details of a defilement.

"The gun he held on us was a 9 mm automatic. Also, I think he knows karate."

Barbara nodded.

"Anything else?"

"I don't think so, except . . ."

His voice trailed off.

"Yes?"

"His whole attitude was mean, sadistic. I got the feeling he was probably glad I jumped at him."

"I see."

Barbara paused.

"This is all good," she said. In fact it wasn't all that good. The only thing new was his observation about Wrigley's knowing karate and the Polo after-shave. Then again, you never knew when seemingly insignificant details could help—even solve a case.

"Anything else?"

"That's all I can remember."

"Fine. This will be very helpful. I hope you get well fast."

Barbara stood up and shook his hand. It was moist.

"I hope you get this bastard," Ketcham said. "He's a real bastard."

"We'll get him."

Barbara turned to go.

"The funny thing is," Ketcham said, "that both Sally and I were raised mostly in the city. We've been out here only about five years. The idea was to get away from all the bad stuff."

He tried to smile.

"I'll never forget what our landlord said," Ketcham went on. "That we'd be safe out here. There are no bad neighborhoods on Long Island."

"That's baloney," Barbara said. "Every place has some danger—it's just a matter of degree."

Ketcham nodded.

"Take care," Barbara said, and then she was gone out the door.

CHAPTER 32

Before he got back to the city from Joplin, Fred Billericks was beeped by his office and told that he had to be in New Orleans within the next twelve hours. There had been a big fire in a department store and arson was suspected.

He barely had time to pack a fresh suitcase full of clothes.

Lawless drove him to Kennedy.

"I'll call you at the station," Billericks said, "as soon as I know when I'll be back. Meanwhile, anything you need in our office, just call—they're ready to help."

"Thanks Fred," Lawless said, "I'll call you if I see something on the horizon."

"Good."

Back at the precinct, there was a message for Lawless from Jack Henry, the artist who was doing the drawing of the man the receptionist at the J & L Clinic had seen.

Lawless called him.

"I'm finished," Henry said. "I think we have him pretty good. At least this Miss Gonzalez thinks so."

"Good. I'll drop over and pick it up."

A half hour later Lawless was in Henry's office looking at the drawing.

As the receptionist had said, the man looked to be close to forty. He was dark haired and had dark eyes.

"He certainly does have weird eyes," Lawless said.

"Yeah, I'm proud of the eyes. When I was drawing the guy the girl wasn't responding too much. But as soon as I nailed those eyes she became alive. She said, 'That's him. That looks a lot like him.'"

"Good," Lawless said, "let's see what we can do with this."

He used Henry's phone to call Bledsoe to find out what the next step was. At least in this instance, defying the higher-ups would have been fruitless.

Lawless explained about the drawing and suggested they get it out to the media.

"I'll have to clear that," Bledsoe said. "Give me your number. I'll call someone and get right back to you."

Five minutes later Bledsoe called back.

"They want us to sit on it for a while," he said.

"Why?" Lawless asked. He was trying to control the surge of anger.

"They don't want to panic people any more than they've already been. This guy is also raising the abortion issue and polarizing people."

"Captain, how do they expect us to work if we can't use our tools?"

"I agree, Lawless," Bledsoe said—it was a rare moment of harmony between the two.

There was a silence. Both men knew the real reason why the brass balked at releasing the drawing: it would point up that no collar had been made; it would broadcast their failure.

"Maybe their feelings will change within the next few days," Bledsoe said.

"Right," Lawless said, "when somebody gets killed." He hung up.

Their feelings would change, he thought, if it suited their purposes—and for no other reason. Catching bad guys was secondary to not risking anything.

Here, too, Lawless thought, a guy like Bledsoe was a mutt. This was the perfect opportunity to go in and fight for something. Logic, reason, and good policework demanded that the suspect be publicized.

But Bledsoe wouldn't do it. He was only concerned with protecting his ass. Once, a long time ago, Flanagan, an old hairbag who Lawless first walked a post with said, "The thing about brass is that in order to get that high they first have to go into the ballroom."

"The ballroom?" Lawless had asked.

"Yeah, that's the room where in exchange for the brass you give them your balls."

It had never seemed truer to Lawless than now.

Sitting at the desk, he lit a cigarette and thought about what to do.

There wasn't much. They knew where the dynamite had been stolen from. They knew it was likely that the perp was a dark-haired man with strange eyes in his late thirties. They knew that he was experienced with dynamite—a pro.

So what?

After finishing the cigarette, Lawless resisted the urge to light another. He figured that in some way the amount you smoked was related to frustration. If he could resist now he would get all the way through.

He stood up.

He did, he thought, have the drawing. Maybe he could show it to someone in the neighborhood of the bombings who might have spotted something. And he could take it around to the other clinics. Maybe someone spotted someone who looked like this guy.

It was worth a shot. But he would need help. He could use a couple of Felony Squad guys, and maybe Billericks could lend him a couple. He would see.

Lawless left the Ivory Tower.

CHAPTER 33

The weather, which had been chilly, turned very cold just about the time Lawless, two guys from the ATF, and two squad guys started going door to door on streets where the clinics were located.

It took three hours to do the canvass around J & L, and by the time Lawless was finished his feet and fingertips were numb.

And he had gotten exactly nowhere. Maybe he wasn't looking for a needle in a haystack—but close enough.

He stopped for a cup of coffee in a luncheonette on the corner of Tremont and Anthony to thaw out and contemplate his next move.

He could think of nothing.

He sipped the coffee, resisted a cigarette, and ordered another coffee.

He thought again: the perp was a pro.

It was not the kind of thing you picked up in a couple of weeks. They didn't give you a case of dynamite and tell you to go out and blast away. You had to know how to handle it safely, but also how much to use.

Lawless remembered what a bomb squad guy had told him once about dynamite.

"It's easy to use too much if you don't know what you're doing. You can intend to blast out some rock formation, and the next thing you know they have to rewrite the guidebooks to the area."

The perp had stolen a case of dynamite. So he could have taken out the entire building—the entire block.

Why didn't he?

Lawless didn't know. But he had no doubt that the perp might blow a whole building yet. You spend years on the street, as Lawless had, and after awhile you got a sense of perps, who they were and what they were about. Lawless wasn't always one hundred percent right, but close. Behavior became very predictable.

He sipped the coffee and glanced around the luncheonette. There were only a few people, and it was hard to see into the street. The front was all plate glass—and heavily frosted.

But where did the perp learn?

Lawless was aware that people who used dynamite had to be certified. Maybe they would find him on the list the dynamite plant manager furnished. Maybe he was a blaster in Joplin. Then again, maybe in New York . . . or a million places in between.

Lawless was sitting at a counter. In the corner of the luncheonette was a phone booth.

He went into it, took out his notebook and dialed Billericks number at the ATF. Miraculously, the phone worked. He got the receptionist, then was connected to McDonald Allen, an agent who worked with Billericks.

"I wanted to know," Lawless asked, "if blasters are registered by the city in which they work."

"Depends on the city," Allen said. "They're under the supervision of the fire department, usually."

"Are there photos?"

"Depends on the city, too. New York has color five-by-seven head shots."

"Good," Lawless said. "I'd like to get a look at whatever they got."

"New York? They got a lot," Allen said. "Their records go back . . ."

"Do you know anyone at the FD who could grease the wheels for me?"

"Sure. Try Terry Rodan—that's a woman. Let me get a number."

MacDonald went off the phone for a moment, then came back on. He gave Lawless the number.

"Good luck."

"Thanks."

Lawless finished his coffee, then went back into the cold. It must have been about zero with the windchill factor.

He got into his car turned the key and it coughed to life. Before he did anything, he would see how the other cops made out with the canvassing.

As he had suspected, none of the other cops had had any luck.

He told his squad people to get back to regular business. The ATF guys went back to whatever they were doing.

Now Lawless would pursue the photograph angle.

The J & L Clinic was not easy to get into. He had to show his shield and prove his identity to two uniformed guards.

That was fine with Lawless. He was glad they were being careful.

After adequately identifying himself, he approached the receptionist's desk.

The woman sitting there was not Gonzalez, the one who had seen the suspect.

Lawless went up to her.

She was heavyset, middle-aged.

"I wonder if you could tell me where Ms. Gonzalez is, the lady who is normally here?"

The woman seemed a little discomfited. Then again, anyone who lived in a ghetto environment tended to view The Man with caution at best, homicidal rage at worst.

"Ponce," the woman said.

That was a big town in Puerto Rico.

"She's on vacation," the woman continued.

"Do you know when she's coming back?"

"Two weeks from tomorrow."

So much for his plan.

"Okay, thanks."

Just on a lark, Lawless slipped the drawing of the

106

perp out of the envelope and showed it to the woman.

"Ever see anyone like this around here?"

She shook her head.

"No."

"Thank you."

Back at the station, Lawless made himself another cup of coffee in the squad room. The coffee he poured for himself was ten times better than the stuff in the luncheonette.

He sat down at one of the desks and leafed through the file.

There were two other squad members at the other desks, one hunt-and-pecking out a report, but it didn't bother Lawless. He had the ability to concentrate in almost any situation.

His idea had been to ask Gonzalez to view the fire department photos. It was an idea that he should have thought of last week, but he hadn't, and he was not overly frustrated by it. It was the nature of investigating.

But he did have one thing—the drawing.

He could use that himself, look at the pictures of blasters and maybe see someone similar.

That could work.

He looked at the drawing.

The guy definitely had a distinctive look. Not just strange eyes. Lawless was looking at a madman.

CHAPTER 34

Johnson knew he better do this right, or that mother-fucking wop could get nasty. And Tiny could get nasty. One mean motherfucker. Kill his mother and pry the gold out of her motherfucking teeth before he dumped her in a lime pit.

Johnson was sitting on a folding chair in the back of a battered black van parked on the southeast corner of Angela and Delaware streets in Philadelphia, an area as isolated as any in Philadelphia, featuring long stretches of cattail fields and auto junkyards, some of them complete with monster vehicle compactors and all with names like Big Joe's and Long Lou's.

It was nine in the morning and cold, with snow on the ground. Though the van protected him against the wind, it did not stop the cold. Every time he exhaled his breath frosted, making Johnson feel colder. He had bought a container of coffee, from which he periodically sipped, but that wasn't doing him much good.

Every now and then Johnson took a hit on a joint. That helped his nerves.

Last time, the problem was that he had not allowed himself enough time. Capezzi had told him to be at the corner at ten o'clock. So he had started out from his rooming house, which was in South Philly, at about 9:30. That should have given him plenty of time.

Except he didn't count on the flat. That fucker had taken him twenty minutes to fix. By the time he got to the corner, they had dropped off the Jag and it had been picked up. He got no pix of the guy who dropped off the car.

When he told Capezzi what happened, Capezzi had

looked at him in a way that made his flesh crawl.

"Don't do it again, Willie," he had said.

Willie was going to make sure he didn't fuck up. He had arrived twenty-five minutes early. He had tested the camera, which had a 750 mm lens—you could see the pimples on someone's ass at three hundred yards.

And Johnson had an alternate plan in the unlikely event someone should park between him and the drop-off point. He would get out and shoot the pix freehand.

He checked his watch.

Nine-fifty. The dudes should be along with the Caddie soon.

He took another deep hit on his roach, felt the pleasant, thick, calming rush, and then carefully extinguished it. He reached in under the heavy coat he was wearing and dropped the roach in the breast pocket of his shirt.

Capezzi, he thought, was a careful and clever motherfucker. That's why he'd never been in jail. A lot of guys who tried to fuck him were in the motherfucking boneyard.

Willie hoped he could do this right.

Frankenstein had an easy time getting the '90 gray Cadillac Eldorado. Stein was driving it and Piccolo was behind in his Trans Am, approaching the corner of Delaware and Hook.

Fazio, a captain in the Gallo family, had not been very careful. Frankenstein had followed him for a couple of hours around where he lived in the Bay Ridge section of Brooklyn. He had gone to an Italian grocery store, an office building—where he had spent an hour but left his bodyguard in the car—and then had driven to a pizza joint where they both went inside.

It was then that Stein moved in. They had left the keys in the car, and it was gone within ten seconds.

Piccolo, who had hung around just to see the show, told Stein what happened later when the two wiseguys came out of the pizza place.

"It beat any kind of entertainment I've been to lately," Piccolo said. "I just wish I had a bag of popcorn while I watched."

First, the confusion over where the car might be, then the kind of frantic going back and forth on the sidewalk, and then the realization: the fucking sting.

Fazio's bodyguard looked scared, as well he might: Fazio would probably end up blaming him for the car's loss.

But watching Fazio's face gradually become the color of his tie, which was red, was too much. Piccolo had exploded in his insane laughter and, as he told Stein when they met up, "I pissed my pants a little. I got to change."

As he approached the appointed corner, Stein noticed the battered van a block away. It meant nothing.

He parked the car as he had done with the Jaguar, then got out and went into the Trans Am and he and Piccolo drove away.

That was it. Simple as pie.

By the time Stein had gotten in the car, Johnson had clicked off thirty-six shots, including four shots of Stein's back as he walked down the block and got into the black Trans Am. Johnson figured the Trans Am was too far away to get anymore good pictures, and it didn't occur to him to try to get the plate number.

Johnson was just interested, now, in getting out of the cold and getting the film processed.

He carefully disassembled the camera and the tripod it was on, and took the roll of film out of the camera. He was going to take it to a one-hour photo lab—and wait.

He fired the van up, and within five blocks he could feel the heater starting to work. He lit the roach and sucked deeply. He was starting to feel good.

* * *

Ten minutes later, a red pickup pulled up alongside the Caddie. Someone got out of the passenger side, got into the Cadillac, fired it up, and a moment later it was heading down the deserted street.

For thirty seconds the street was empty; the only sign of life under the gray, cold sky was steam drifting up from a manhole far in the distance.

Thirty seconds later, the black Trans Am turned back onto the street. Inside was Frankenstein, Piccolo driving.

The gray Cadillac was out of sight, but Frankenstein, who was following it, was not concerned.

In the center of the console was a small gray metal box with a light green screen. Every second a yellow dot pulsed to life, like the cursor on a computer screen.

The device was picking up signals emitted by a bumper beeper, commonly called a bird dog by cops, which Frankenstein had secured with alnico magnets under the left rear bumper of the Cadillac. As long as Frankenstein stayed within two miles, they would not lose it.

Twenty minutes later, Frankenstein approached a big factory-like building that was like all the others on the block and faced the pier of the Philadelphia port.

The car was nowhere in sight, but the bird dog said it had been driven inside the building.

"We'll come back later," Piccolo said, "for a better look."

CHAPTER 35

Johnson waited for the pictures, which were ready about noon.

He was happy. Every shot, except one, came out. They showed the big redheaded guy very clearly.

It occurred to Johnson with a sinking sensation that maybe he should have gotten a picture of the Trans Am. It didn't show in any of the pictures. What Tiny didn't know wouldn't hurt him.

Johnson headed over to Capezzi headquarters in South Philadephia immediately.

The headquarters certainly didn't look like much. It was a white, blue-trimmed, scarred and battered mobile home, set on cinder blocks at the entrance to the Union Auto Parts yard, more popularly known as Tiny's, which was, in fact, a legitimate junkyard, complete with equipment for reducing a car to the size of a TV cabinet.

The place was in keeping with Angelo Capezzi's over-all philosophy: lay low.

He never stopped saying he was a legitimate businessman, and had refused hundreds of interviews with the media down through the years. To him, publicity was the plague. He explained it to someone once.

"You see, if you make yourself well known, every hump in the world is going to try to nail your ass because it makes him look good. It's like a kid wanting to cut down a big gunfighter. And while we're all smart guys, sooner or later we make mistakes. If you got law enforcement looking up your ass twenty-four hours a day, they're going to be there when you make a mistake. Do everything you can to keep out of the limelight and you'll stay out of jail."

Capezzi's office was on one end of the mobile home and Capezzi, who could invariably be found behind a desk there, seemed to be almost as wide as the home.

His nickname, out of earshot of course, was Tiny Capezzi.

He was bald, with bulging eyes, and thick lips and had very bad skin from acne when a kid, which still occasionally flared up.

He weighed about four hundred pounds and was, said one cop, "pound for pound the meanest Mafioso who ever waddled down the pike."

Contrary to the image that fat people are jolly, Capezzi never smiled—except when an enemy was in pain.

Johnson came into the mobile home at about one o'clock.

A couple of men, who weighed close to six hundred pounds between them and in no way resembled missionaries, escorted him to Capezzi.

"I got the pictures, Mr. Capezzi," Johnson said, feeling about three years old.

Capezzi, who was seated, put out a pudgy hand. Johnson handed the pictures to him.

Capezzi leafed through them.

There was no reaction, and that was how Johnson could tell he was pleased. When he didn't get pissed he was pleased.

"Pay the man his money," Capezzi said to one of the apes.

One big man peeled off some bills and handed then to Johnson.

Johnson's eyes were alight as the bills were being peeled off, but he followed the count and said to the man; "Excuse me. There's only three hundred there. Mr. Capezzi promised me four hundred dollars."

Capezzi spoke.

"Three hundred is right. You fucked up first time. I'm fining you a hundred for that."

Johnson felt a river of rage forming in him. He nodded.

"Oh," he said. "Okay." And added, "Thank you." He didn't want Capezzi to detect any disrespect. That could get him a quick trip to the bone orchard.

He left.

After he did, Capezzi handed the pictures to the ape who had given Johnson the money. The ape's name was Aldo.

"Go," he said.

Three hours later, Aldo was tooling through New York in his own Caddie, down Houston Street in downtown Manhattan. He pulled the car over to a bar called Danny's and parked.

He went into the bar, which was a typical neighborhood place.

At the bar itself were some hard-looking drinkers, five or six men and two older women. Along the left side there were tables and some booths.

Aldo approached one of the booths in back. Sitting in it was a heavyset, middle-aged man with a reddish face and stark white hair, neatly trimmed and combed. He was wearing a sport shirt and slacks, and he looked like a cop, which in fact he used to be.

Aldo sat down opposite him.

He handed him two envelopes, one of which contained the pictures, the other a wad of cash.

"If he's sour," Aldo said, "Mr. Capezzi wants to work under the usual bonus arrangement, okay?"

The man nodded.

He knew what it was: double the fee if he found out that the thief was undercover. That's how he had doubled his fee on the last guy.

CHAPTER 36

The day after she spoke to the latest male victim, Ketcham, Barbara Babalino stayed late at the station. Over the last twenty-four hours plenty of new business had come, which had pulled her efforts away from the Wrigley's case.

So, as soon as she got the chance, she was determined to look at the file material again, to see if she could get a lead of any sort.

The first chance she got was at ten o'clock that night. She cleared her desk, got a cup of coffee, and sat down with the material.

In any bureaucracy a single case can pile up paperwork fast. When there are multiple crimes, from multiple jurisdictions, the paperwork can be quite extensive.

She had a nine-inch pile to go through.

As she glanced at the reports she had written, it occurred to her how effectively they hid the human stories. DD 5s reported facts; they did not tell you that someone named Joan Keenan would likely spend the rest of her life in a mental institution because of her rape and desertion by her fiancé.

They did not tell you about the shame and horror someone named Bobby O'Rourke felt—and how it would probably stay with him the rest of his life.

Barbara proceeded slowly and methodically through the files.

As she went, she tried to summon up images of the people and places that she wrote about. There were always so many more details that the reports excluded. You could say a person had red hair, for example, but you could not say in the report how the hair was carrot red, or was particularly glossy—or whatever.

But your mind recorded everything. Barbara had read somewhere that people received one hundred thousand impressions a second, all instantly processed and stored in the brain.

It took her forty-five minutes to leaf through everything, and then she rubbed her eyes and leaned back in her chair.

As with any crime, she was looking for connections. Every crime reflected, to one degree or another, an image of the perp.

What did these crimes tell her?

Certainly that he was savage, vicious—and unusual. There was probably a gay component in his personality, though it was not dominant.

She thought about that awhile.

It didn't lead her anywhere.

There was no connection . . . .

Did the victims know each other?

She and Bickford had asked that. They didn't. There was no connection whatsoever.

Except that as victims they fell into a very narrow profile.

All were white, young, and lived together. Three were from Long Island and one from Siberia.

Barbara sipped her coffee.

The crimes had occurred over a three-month period. Wrigley's had been able to find victims, track them, and do them fairly quickly.

Barbara thought there were many young couples—a mass of victims, you might say—to select from. It was not as if they were from a small group.

Barbara stood up and stretched.

Her stomach tightened and she felt a surge of sadness as she thought of Joan Keenan.

Yes, her life was over.

Barbara wondered what would have happened if she had not been raped.

Something bad. She was so fragile. Yet people who are fragile can go their entire lives without bad problems if their situations stay stable.

She recalled Jake Ketcham's words: "Our landlord said that we'd be safe out here." No matter what precautions you took, you could never really be secure.

She sifted through her memory and returned to the interview with Joan Keenan; she too had mentioned a landlord. "Pallone isn't the best . . . Doesn't do all he should."

A question occurred to Barbara.

All the victims' homes were alike—who were the landlords of the other buildings? Maybe there was a connection there. Maybe this Pallone knew them all.

No, that didn't make sense: the victims would recognize him.

Idly, Barbara leafed through the files.

There was no indication that she could see of who the landlord was in any of the other houses.

Barbara came across the name of Jeanie Ryan, the spunky young girl.

Her number was there.

Barbara glanced at her watch. It was close to eleven. Not that late.

Barbara dialed Jeanie Ryan's number.

After two rings a male voice answered.

"Yeah?"

"Hello, this is Detective Babalino. Is Jeanie Ryan there?"

"Hold on."

Jeanie Ryan came on.

"I was just wondering," Barbara said, "if you could give me the name of your landlord."

"Sure," Jeanie Ryan said. "Pallone. David Pallone."

Barbara said nothing for a moment. Her heart was hammering.

"Do you know where he lives?"

"He has an office on Pulaski Road in Huntington, Long Island. Do you want the address?"

"Please."

Jeanie Ryan went off the phone a moment, then came back and gave Barbara the address.

Barbara thanked her and hung up.

She had the breakthrough—but she made the other calls anyhow. It was, she thought, pro forma.

She only reached Ketcham, but his one-word answer said it all: "Pallone."

CHAPTER 37

Barbara and Bickford were sitting in their car outside 387 Pulaski Road the next morning at 8:30. They had arrived at 7:30 and had tried the door to the building, a one-story, flat-roofed brick type, but there was no answer and it was locked.

From the signs outside in the front there appeared to be three tenants in the building: an insurance company, a Gestalt psychology clinic, and David Pallone, Inc.

At around eight o'clock a middle-aged heavyset blond woman had driven into the rear parking lot and apparently entered the building.

At 8:15, a young, modishly dressed man driving a white Corvette had driven into the parking lot, and a few minutes later another middle-aged woman, this one with dark hair, had driven to the back.

As time went by, the detectives knew, more and more people would arrive, but they thought they would recognize Pallone if he showed up. Bickford had done some homework on Pallone, and had gotten a duplicate of his driver's license, complete with picture, which he showed to Barbara.

He was a short, dark-haired forty-three-year-old,

who had no yellow sheet but had his share of tickets from DMV. He had a bad habit of accumulating moving violations, and his license had been suspended twice over the last ten years.

His residence was at 120 Spencer Street in Northport, which Bickford told Barbara was about fifteen minutes from his office.

His home and office were within ten minutes of the houses where two of the assaults had occurred.

It was decided that if Pallone showed up, both detectives would approach him. They didn't anticipate trouble any more than cops always did. Any situation could quickly escalate from being mild and routine to dangerous—or deadly.

At 8:40 a black Corvette that both cops knew was Pallone's pulled off Pulaski and went up a driveway adjacent to the building to the rear parking lot. The cops got out of their vehicle and crossed Pulaski, which was a very busy road, particularly now in the rush hour.

Without a word, Barbara had put her .38 special in the pocket of the long coat she was wearing, and Bickford had loosened both his coat and his suit jacket so he could get to his gun quickly if need be.

They intersected with Pallone as he turned away from his car after locking it.

He looked startled, wary.

"Mr. Pallone?" Bickford said.

"Yes."

"I'm Jack Bickford with the Suffolk police. We'd like to have a word with you."

Pallone looked startled.

"What about?"

"Can we go inside?"

Pallone's brow furrowed, but he said nothing. He opened a back door with a key and the detectives followed him inside.

They went down a short, tiled hall, past three offices, one of which was occupied the blond middle-aged woman. There was no sign of the other people who had entered the building.

Pallone's office was about the size of a living room, larger than the others.

The office decor was modern, and there were a couple of framed color photos on the walls showing people posed in front of small racing cars. A bookshelf held a couple of small trophies, though Barbara could not tell if they were for racing.

Pallone went behind his desk, but he did not sit down.

"What's this all about?"

"It's about rape," Bickford said. "Over the last three months, four couples have been raped in apartments owned by you. Have you heard anything about them?"

Color drained from Pallone's face.

"I heard about one. Ketcham," he said. "What were the others?"

Barbara detailed them.

A little color came back into Pallone's cheeks. Just enough to make then looked blotchy.

"So what do you want from me?" he asked. His eyes challenged, flicking first to Bickford, then to Barbara.

The detectives said nothing for a moment. Then Bickford spoke.

"Who else had access to your records besides you?"

Pallone's eyes lowered, then raised.

"No one . . . except I get an office temp in here to work occasionally."

"How often do you do this?" Barbara asked.

"When the work piles up enough."

"Any of them male?" Barbara asked.

"One."

"What's his name?"

"I forget."

"Do you have the names of these people?" Bickford asked.

"No."

"How could we get 'em?" Bickford asked.

"I don't know. Contact the temporary companies."

Bickford spoke. There was an edge to his voice.

"You know, Mr. Pallone, this is a police investigation. I sense that you don't want to cooperate. We'd like *you* to get the names of everyone who's worked here on a temporary basis over the last six months."

"That's a lot of work."

"Maybe," Bickford said, "but if I were you I'd get on this case for another reason."

"What's that?"

"Litigation," Bickford said. "You could be facing some lawsuits."

Pallone blinked.

"Why?"

"A lawyer could say you didn't provide adequate security."

Pallone said nothing.

"Okay, I'll get the names."

"When will you have 'em?" Bickford asked.

"The next day or so."

"Here's my number," Bickford said. "Call."

As they drove away, Bickford said, "I think he'll cooperate fully. You always have to take a macho man like that down a peg."

"You did."

"Do you think he might be the perp?"

"I don't know. I don't think so. That was the sense I got."

There was a silence for a while.

"Did you," Barbara finally said, "get a feeling he was holding back, or lying?"

"Sort of—but it's hard to be sure."

"I don't know. There was one time when he lowered his eyes, when we asked him who had access to the records."

"I didn't notice that. I just got a general feeling he was holding back. Of course, most people do anyway."

"Yeah," Barbara said.

"We'll just have to see what he comes up with. I'll give him until tomorrow night, then we'll see." Bickford said.

"Right."

CHAPTER 38

At around eleven o'clock the day after they met with Pallone, Bickford called Barbara, who was at the station in her cubicle going over business from the night before.

"Pallone called," Bickford said. "He came up with two office temps. They work for the same company. I called the company and they are on assignment in the area. Can you come out now? We might be able to catch 'em on their lunch hour."

Barbara had a two o'clock court appearance, but everything else was standard Siberia.

"Where and when?"

They arranged to meet at the Whitman Mall in Huntington at around noon. That's where one of the people was working.

The temporary was a twenty-three-year-old man named Alan Maguire who was working in the offices of A&S.

Both detectives knew they were flying in the dark. Ideally, it would have been best if they had called and arranged an appointment with Maguire. But that would have given him advance notice they were coming.

They got lucky.

Maguire was there when they arrived, having a sandwich at his desk, which was actually a large artist's easel in the art room.

Maguire was a short, thin man with blond hair and

a pale complexion. He had large brown eyes and, though Barbara knew he was only twenty-three, he looked perhaps five years older.

He seemed very nervous when they identified themselves. Barbara suspected that he might be gay.

Barbara tried to reassure Maguire, who had not risen from his desk during the introductions.

"We're just here," she said, "to ask you a couple of questions about your work with Mr. Pallone."

Maguire blinked as if he was trying to remember, then remembered.

"All right."

"When did you work for him?" Barbara asked.

"About five months ago."

"How long?"

"Just a month or so. He needed help in preparing ads for apartments and the like."

"Where did the ads go?" Bickford asked.

"Mostly in Nassau and Suffolk, a few in the Bronx."

"Why just a few in the Bronx?" Barbara asked.

"Mr. Pallone only had a few apartments there."

There was a pause.

"What kind of response did you get to the ads?" Barbara asked.

"We got a lot of responses. Mr. Pallone was happy with the work I did."

"Did you get to interview the couples?"

"No. Mr. Pallone did that. I just did pasteup."

"Would they come to the office?" Barbara asked.

"Yes."

"Did you know who rented and who did not?" Bickford asked.

He shook his head.

"No," he said.

They talked to Maguire a few more minutes. On the face of it, it did not appear that he had anything to do with the assaults.

They thanked him and, after telling him that they

might want to speak with him again, they left. Barbara could tell that he was very relieved that, at least for now, they were through with him.

The other office temp's name was Anna Marcella. She was working in a big bank near the Hicksville train station.

Bickford and Barbara got lucky there, too. Marcella's lunch break was at one o'clock. They arrived at around 1:20.

Anna Marcella was a small, pretty woman, who seemed to have taken great care in applying her makeup, which seemed a touch overdone to Barbara; a little too much of everything. It definitely didn't have a natural look; it was almost as if she was wearing a mask.

Barbara and Bickford found her in a small private cafeteria that served the bank's workers. She told them that she would talk with them outside, where she could smoke a cigarette. They followed her.

They asked her all the questions they had posed to Maguire, and it seemed that she, like Maguire, had nothing to do with the people who rented the apartments, though she did see them come into the office. Her only job was to input data about Pallone's various businesses.

"So you never knew who rented what?" Bickford asked.

"I did—because I input the information—but I wasn't really that interested in it."

"Oh," Bickford said.

Marcella took a deep drag on her cigarette. She grimaced a bit, as if the cigarette tasted bad. But it wasn't the cigarette. It was a memory.

"I didn't work there that long, anyway," she said. "I didn't like it that much. Particularly with that creep around."

"Who?" Barbara asked.

"Brad," Marcella said. "Brad Fusari. He was Mr. Pallone's nephew or something."

"Why is he a creep?" Barbara asked. "What did he do?"

"Nothing. I mean I only saw him a few times. He did maintenance jobs on Mr. Pallone's houses. He was, uh, good looking. But it was just the way he looked at me."

"What do you mean?"

"Well, for example, once I was working at the VDT and I sensed that someone was watching me. When I turned around I saw Brad. He had a very strange look in his eyes, and I thought he even might be smiling."

"What does he look like?" Bickford asked.

"Short, muscular, dark hair and eyes. Handsome . . . looks a little like the actor Ralph Macchio."

"I don't know him," Bickford said.

"I do," Barbara said. "Did you ever speak with him?"

"He said hello to me, but I just didn't want to get involved."

"Do you know where he is now?" Bickford asked.

"No. Mr. Pallone should. Like I said, he's his nephew."

Bickford looked at Barbara.

CHAPTER 39

Forty-five minutes after they left Anna Marcella, Bickford and Barbara entered the Pulaski Road offices of Pallone. They went in through the rear entrance, as they had in the morning.

They went down the hall to his office. He was sitting

behind his desk and was startled by their appearance, then seemingly annoyed.

Pallone looked as if he were about to say something. But Bickford, with Barbara behind him, spoke first.

"Who's Brad Fusari, Mr. Pallone?" he said.

Pallone blinked rapidly. He glanced first at Bickford, then Barbara.

"My nephew. My sister's boy."

"He work here?" Barbara asked.

"Not anymore."

"When did he start to work here?" Barbara asked.

Pallone blinked even more rapidly. His complexion was mottled.

"Maybe two or three months ago."

"Steady?"

"Off and on."

"For how long?"

"I don't know. Maybe a month."

"What'd he do?" Barbara asked.

"Odd jobs."

"Where does he live?" Bickford asked.

"I don't know."

"You don't know where he lives?" Barbara asked.

"He used to live with my sister. I also let him sleep in some of the vacant apartments. I don't know where he is now."

"When is the last time you saw him?" Barbara asked.

"I don't know. Maybe three weeks ago."

The questioning had been rapid fire. Now there was a lull. The detectives stared at Pallone.

"What do you want with him?" Pallone said.

"He may be a suspect," Bickford said.

"Not a chance! He's a good boy."

Pallone seemed on the verge of saying something else, but said nothing.

"Where does your sister live?" Barbara asked.

"Centerport."

Barbara turned to Bickford.

"That's near here," Bickford said.

"Can we have the address?" Barbara asked.

"Hey," Pallone said, "don't go bothering my sister. She's had enough grief in her life."

"What do you mean?" Barbara asked.

"Just don't go bothering her."

Pallone looked at them in a challenging way.

"All we want is her address," Barbara said. "Sooner or later we'll get it—whether or not you give it to us."

Pallone gave them the address. They left the office. Pallone watched them go.

Outside, they got into the car.

"I'd bet anything this kid is the perp," Bickford said.

"Looks good."

"Pallone knows, too."

Barbara nodded as Bickford started up the car. A moment later they were out of the parking lot and heading down Pulaski toward Centerport.

When the detectives had started questioning him about Brad, David Pallone's mind had gone blank, because he knew right away what it was. Brad had given nothing but grief to his sister, Alma, since he was young.

Now he knew he was going to give her more grief.

Pallone ground his teeth. He was such a little bastard. He had so tried to help him. He should have died a long time ago.

Pallone got up and lit a cigarette. He looked at the phone console sitting on his desk.

He hated the idea of calling Alma.

He went over to his door and closed it, then went back to the phone. He picked up the phone and dialed the number.

It rang once.

"Hello."

"It's Dave," he said. "How are you?"

"All right. Okay."

There was a moment's hesitation.

"Where's Brad?"

"In his room."

"I just talked with two cops. They're on their way over there to see him, I think."

"Oh God!"

"Maybe he didn't do anything. There's always the chance of that."

"I can't talk now, Dave. I . . . I'll call you later."

CHAPTER 40

Bickford knew the area well, so it only took him and Barbara ten minutes to get to Pallone's sister's house.

The house was on a narrow street that was flanked by trees. All of the lawns in the neighborhood were well cared for—except the sister's.

The house was set far back from the road. An uneven path of patio blocks led to it.

The house looked dilapidated. It was white, but had not been painted in a long time. Paint was peeling, parts of the roofing were curled back, and the gutter was askew.

In sum, it was an eyesore.

"The neighbors must love this place," Bickford said as he and Barbara walked up the driveway.

"Yeah, funny place for a handyman to live," she said.

They climbed five concrete steps, all of which were cracked, and rang the doorbell. It didn't work. Bickford knocked.

After thirty seconds or so, the door opened.

A woman stood in the doorway. It was hard to tell her age, but Barbara guessed she was about fifty.

She had bleached blond hair, which was gray at the roots, a very wrinkled face, and used too much makeup. Her lipstick was startlingly red.

The body didn't go with the face. It was the shapely body of a younger woman. She wore a pink sweater that emphasized her breasts, which were largish. She had a cigarette in her right hand.

She had china-blue, rheumy eyes.

"Yeah?" she said.

"We're looking for Bradley Fusari." Bickford said.

"Who are you?" The woman asked.

"We're police officers," Bickford said. "Who are you?"

"I'm his mother," she said, and took a deep drag on the cigarette.

Barbara realized something about the woman. There was a certain air she had, a certain control. Pallone probably warned her they were coming.

"Why do you want to see him?"

"An assault case," Bickford said.

The woman said nothing. She was a tough cookie.

"Is he here now?" Barbara asked.

"No, he ain't. He ain't been here for a while."

"When do you expect him back?"

The woman held her hands out as if to say, Who knows?

"Where does he work?" Bickford asked.

"He does odd jobs. He works everywhere—and nowhere."

Barbara glanced at Bickford. They weren't going to get anything from her.

Bickford took a card from his jacket pocket and handed it to the woman.

"If he shows up, ask him to contact us, will you?"

"Sure," the woman said.

Barbara handed her her card. Some perps would talk to a female cop. It was worth the shot.

An hour later, Bickford and Barbara were back in Bickford's office in Huntington. Bickford had fed Bradley Fusari's name into Central ID to see whether he had a yellow sheet.

A half an hour later, they learned that he did. Walker, a guy who worked in communications, came into Bickford's office, where he and Barbara were having coffee.

"He's a got a sheet all right," Walker said. "And he's on parole."

"For what?"

"Rape."

Bickford called Fusari's parole officer and was told he was in the field and that he would probably be returning before the end of the day.

Bickford and Barbara decided that it was best for Barbara to return to the Five Three to do other business. As soon as Bickford heard from the parole officer, he would contact her.

Barbara was in her office at six that night when Bickford called.

"I got through to the parole guy," he said. "Fusari's been on parole for three months."

"About the time the assaults started."

"That's right. But the MO varies."

"How so?"

"The parole guy said he was suspected of attacking a series of single women in the Northport area, but they only got him for one assault. A thirty-year-old nurse. But he beat her up pretty bad."

"So he only started with couples since he got out?"

"As far as they know."

"We got another problem. Bad one."

"What's that?"

"He's HIV positive."

Barbara said nothing for a moment. Pallone had the precursor to AIDS.

"For sure?"

"They tested him in prison."

130

"Jesus."

"Yeah," Bickford said, "we got to find this guy."

Quickly, Barbara thought. Because now it was a question not only of raping couples, but of sentencing them to death. For all intents and purposes, he might already have killed the four couples they knew about.

And maybe some people they didn't know about.

CHAPTER 41

Leo Molinari looked out the window.

It was cold, clear, the sky light gray. The only sign of life was smoke coming from factory stacks in the distance, which just peeked over a line of private homes.

It was the sunless kind of day he hated when he was a kid, the kind of day when he always seemed to be waiting, waiting. . . .

He closed his eyes briefly. Feelings returned. The hollow, empty feeling that Mother was not around. The feeling of fear as he waited for her to come home from work. The hoping that she would come home alone.

For some reason, he remembered a day like this just before his tenth birthday.

As usual, his mother had left him in the house to watch his eight brothers and sisters, who were all younger, while she went to her job at Rogers Brothers Restaurant.

He wanted her to come home very much, but he was afraid, too.

Sometimes when she came home she would get mad at him for what the other kids had done. She held him responsible for everything everyone did, because he was the oldest.

"Oh Leo," she would scream at him, "can't I ever depend on you?"

He also never knew if she was going to bring a "friend" home. His mother had brought many different friends home as he grew up. Some of them seemed nice, but he never liked any of them, and he would hate it when she would go upstairs to her bedroom with them and he would hear them making noise in the bed.

He had never met his own father. Mother told him that his father had left her before he was born. Some of his brothers and sisters had met their fathers, but none of the fathers ever stayed for long. He remembered one "friend" named Charley stayed for about a year, but that was the longest his mother had even been with a man.

Molinari turned from the window and sat down at the kitchen table.

If anyone had a right to destroy life it was him, Leo Molinari. Why bring life into a world where mothers don't care?

He laced his delicate fingers together.

Almost all of his brothers and sisters had perished in one way or another. Some were drunks, others dope users. Two were in prison. Two were dead.

Only one, besides himself, his sister Anne, who was a nun, had survived. They survived because they had found the love of the Lord, and the Lord's love included all living creatures, no matter how small or how malformed.

He remembered part of a line from one of the books of the novelist Thomas Wolfe: "In her dark womb we did not know our mother's face."

How could they say that in the womb nothing was alive, just because what was in it did not look human, or was too small to be readily observable?

The life was there. The soul. The soul was the first thing that formed; the conjunction of egg and sperm occurred, and by the miracle of conception a human soul was formed.

The body was a mere container, the package that *contained* the soul.

All over the world, souls were dying.

Molinari's eyes filled with tears.

And they are not listening, he thought. Not listening to the voice of humanity, the voice of reason, the voice of God.

Stop killing our babies.

Anger surged, white hot.

He stood up. *If they will not listen, I will make them listen. I will teach them a lesson that they will never, ever forget.*

Molinari seethed. He would not wait much longer.

CHAPTER 42

The guy at the fire department had a sense of humor. He told Joe Lawless that there were not 2500 photos of blasters—"just 2456."

Lawless did not appreciate the humor, though he said nothing. The guy had no idea what the cops were up against. Or what was at stake.

The guy found a conference room for Lawless to use and he went through the photographs, which were in ten piles, methodically, looking at each so he could make, in as many cases as possible, a determination on whether it looked anything like the sketch.

There were many photographs that he could immediately put aside as not looking anything like the suspect. People with large ears, protruding noses or other features that did not begin to be reflected in the drawing.

Then there were others that were not that close, but

not far enough away so that he could immediately stop considering them.

Then there were others, not many, that he thought were fairly close; at least they bore much closer examination.

As he went, he looked frequently at the drawing, and after awhile it almost seemed as if the drawing were alive: the dark, insane eyes smiled at him. Once near the end of the day, he thought one of the eyes winked at him.

After ten hours, he had eliminated the bulk of the photos, and started to concentrate on some thirty that were left.

He slowly eliminated ten of these, and then was left with a final twenty.

Before he looked again at these, he took—after eleven hours—his first break, just to rest his eyes and have a bite and a cigarette, only his third of the day.

That was quite good. A year ago if he had been involved in an investigation with this much pressure he would have, after eleven hours, been working on his third pack.

It was pretty cold out, but after all that time cooped up in a room Lawless didn't notice. It was bracing, refreshing, and had the desired effect: it cleared his head, resharpened his eye.

There was no place nearby where he could get a bite, so he just had a cigarette and went back into the room.

As he went over the final twenty photos, some of them seemed wrong, and he set those aside. But he did not consider them totally dead.

Finally, he was left with nine photos, all of which, he thought, were close enough to the drawing to have the receptionist look at. And he had dreamt up a way to do that fast—fax them to Ponce. A friend named Hector Robles worked for the Ponce cops.

Three of the men had mustaches and six did not. Seven of the nine had hair that was dark, ranging from dirty brown to black; the other two had blond hair.

Lawless had disregarded hair color as well as facial hair in looking at the photos. The suspect could well have disguised himself.

What he mainly focused on were the eyes. A certain look, a certain wildness, a certain madness. It occurred to Lawless that of 2500 men who were certified to use dynamite, more than one could have a couple of screws loose.

At around midnight, Lawless left the facility and headed over to One Police Plaza.

In an envelope were the photos of the nine men he thought most looked like the drawing.

At eleven o'clock, copies of the photos had been faxed to Robles in Ponce.

Lawless had also been able to reach Gonzalez, through the receptionist at her hotel. She had agreed to go over and look at the pictures, but it was hard getting a cab that late at night.

Lawless said that he would have someone pick her up.

After he spoke with her he talked to Robles again, and Robles told him, "No problem, amigo. I'll pick her up and watch her while she looks. Then we'll call."

Lawless had given the witness his number at One Police Plaza, but he also gave it to Robles. He didn't want any mess-ups because of a wrong number.

He then got himself a cup of coffee, had only his sixth cigarette of the day—but his second in the last hour—and sat down in an office he had borrowed from a safe and loft squad guy he knew named Doug Adams.

As he waited, Lawless thought about what he might do if the witness couldn't ID anyone in the photos.

Not much. They would be playing a waiting game, waiting for the bomber to strike again. Then they would investigate the scene and, hopefully, come up with new evidence.

Meanwhile, someone might be killed.

But he had the feeling that it was one of the people he had picked out. Of the nine he had winnowed the search to, he felt that three looked pretty close to the drawing.

And one, number four, looked very close.

All the coloring on this man was wrong. The perp had been dark haired, and number four had light hair.

But it was the eyes that got him.

They were intense dark, and . . . crazy. He was not imagining that into the picture because of the case. He truly thought the eyes were crazy.

C2azy and very much like the eyes in the drawing. The eyes were so distinctive, the ID could almost be made by them alone.

Lawless was about to go out of the office when the phone, which was on the desk where he had been sitting, rang.

He picked up.

The sound was staticky. Long distance.

A man spoke.

"Joe Lawless?" The man said.

"This is Joe Lawless."

"It's Robles, Joe. Your witness wants to speak with you."

There was a temporary pause.

"Oh, Mr. Lawless," Ivette Gonzalez said, "I looked at the pictures. It's number four. That's the man who came in that day."

"Are you sure? He's got blond hair."

"The eyes," she said. "I'll never forget his eyes."

Inside, Lawless soared. But self-control, developed through years of experience, automatically kicked in.

"Thank you," he said, "thank you very much. Please put Detective Robles back on."

Robles came back on.

"Thanks Hector, I really appreciate it."

"*Vaya con Dios*," Robles said. "*Buen suerte*."

Lawless hung up and sat back down at the desk.

He looked at the picture of number four. He didn't need to read the make sheet on the back.

The guy's name was Leo Molinari.

CHAPTER 43

Around eleven o'clock on the night of the day they dropped off the Cadillac, Frankenstein parked Piccolo's Trans Am far down the street and started walking toward the warehouse-like building.

It was very cold, but there was no wind coming off the water, and that helped. They were warmly dressed and looked, with their woolen pullover caps, like seamen.

Under the long coats both wore soft body armor and were loaded for bear. Stein had a sawed-off shotgun in addition to a 9 mm fourteen-shot automatic, while Piccolo had an alley gun, so called because it was said its shot pattern could take down everyone in an alley, and his .44 Magnum—"in case we have to blow a hole through a wall to get in."

Getting in, it had been determined by Frankenstein, was not going to be that easy—or even looking in, for that matter.

Earlier they had cased the joint by car, driving in and around it. There were two entrances in the front—a big swing-up garage door and a regular door—plus one entrance on the side.

There were a number of large windows, but they were apparently all shut tight and sealed; some sort of dark material had been taped on the inside so no one could look in.

Frankenstein assumed that there was someone inside,

but they couldn't be sure. There were a few cars parked across the road, but there was no way to know if they belonged to anyone inside the building.

Briefly, they had considered trying to get inside the building, but had decided against it. If there was someone there that would mean a confrontation, and they didn't want that. For one thing, the warehouse was out of their jurisdiction, and there would be all kinds of questions as to just how Frankenstein had found out about it. What were two cops from the fifty-third precinct in New York doing on a street in Philadelphia?

Frankenstein decided that the best thing to do was just observe what was inside the building—hopefully, a lot of cars and trucks. Then they could decide what to do from that point. It might be as simple as dropping a dime to the Philadelphia cops.

The cold was good for Frankenstein. It kept the streets empty except for an occasional car that came down Delaware.

It was a dark night, and artificial lighting was not that good either. There was an old-fashioned lamppost far across the road that illuminated the parking area by the docks, but that was about it. The building itself was in virtual darkness.

As they approached the building, Frankenstein did not speak, and they became particularly attuned to any sound that might come from inside the building. There was none.

To the right of the building was an alley that separated the building from another of similar construction. They knew from their drive-by that there were no lights in it.

Just before they turned down it they glanced every which way to make sure no one was watching.

The windows on the building were black rectangles within the larger blackness of the building.

Frankenstein was looking for one thing: a sliver of

light in a window. That would mean a gap where they could look in.

There appeared to be a gap in the next to last window from the rear of the building.

They stopped and looked each way.

Then Stein got down on his haunches and Piccolo got on his shoulders, his legs draped over his neck.

"First floor, please," Piccolo said.

Stein stood up, then grabbed Piccolo by the behind and lifted him above his head.

"Oh," Piccolo said, "you turn me on!"

"Don't make me laugh, Frank! I'll drop you!" Piccolo, holding onto the wall to steady himself, eventually got his feet on Stein's shoulders.

That was fine.

He got his face as close to the glass as he could so that he could look through the BB-sized hole in whatever material was covering the window.

He looked for thirty seconds.

"Down, please."

Stein lowered him to the ground.

"Pay dirt," he said. "That fucking place is loaded with cars and trucks—and I think I saw my nephew's."

"Terrific," Stein said, and they walked out of the alley, looked both ways down Delaware, then were gone.

CHAPTER 44

Ten minutes after they had paid a visit to the building, Frankenstein was sitting in a back booth in an all-night diner on Franklin Street. There were only a few other people. Each had ordered coffee.

Piccolo took a long drag on a cigarette.

"Whatever we do," he said, "we got to do it fast. They got to be ready to move. That warehouse is loaded to the gills."

"What do you figure, Frank, drop a dime to the Philadelphia cops?"

"That's one way. I'd want to make sure the cop we go to is clean."

"I know a cop named Spagnoli in the Chester police—a suburb. Maybe he knows someone."

"That's an idea. We could also get the state involved."

"Right."

"It's a fucking shame we can't get Capezzi."

"I was thinking about that. All we can hope is that they flip somebody after the bust."

A waitress brought their coffee over.

"One good thing," Piccolo said, "there's no chance the Ferret can get involved."

"That's right. Just drop the dime."

"Yeah, but we should tell him to keep up that wop contact. If he disappears just before they get busted they'll smell a fucking rat."

"That's right."

"We'll have to stay involved also."

"Yeah."

"But we'll want to stay away from where we can get busted."

"That right."

They sipped the coffee in silence.

"It's a shame," Stein said, "we can't get credit for this."

Piccolo smiled.

"Hey Howie, nothing could help us. We could save the pope from being sodomized by a gorilla and it wouldn't amount to a hill of shit against our folders."

"I guess."

"So," Piccolo said, "we'll do it first thing in the morning. Drop a dime to your friend in Chester. They'll probably want to set up surveillance, make the bust all at once."

"If they do it right."

"By that time, too," Stein said, "we can dream up some baloney story on how we got on to it. They'll want to listen."

"Fuckin' A."

CHAPTER 45

At around the time that Frankenstein was having coffee in the all-night diner, Tiny Capezzi was sitting in his mobile-home office on Penrose Street. On the desk in front of him was a pepperoni pizza—or what was left. He was slowly eating the eighth and last slice.

Sitting in front of Tiny on a straight-backed chair, flanked by two gorillas, was the Ferret. He was in his underwear, shivering, gooseflesh the size of peas on his arms even though it was warm in the office.

The Ferret knew his life was on the line. They had picked him up off the streets in New York three hours earlier and brought him here. Then they had stripped him to see if he was wearing a wire. That was a very bad sign: they didn't trust him.

The Ferret knew that his only hope was to play out the string. Admit nothing. Act. It had to be the performance of his life, or . . .

"Tell me again where you met this guy," Capezzi said after taking a big swallow and dabbing his mouth with a napkin.

The Ferret had his cover story all ready, even before the two goons had grabbed him.

"I knew him from around Finnegan's, a bar where I hang out. He was always doing bets, betting pretty heavy on the ponies, and I used to have a drink with him every now and then. I knew he was into swag for a long time."

"Stealing what?"

"Cars, jewelry . . . lots of different stuff."

"So you figured he was straight?"

"Yeah. He is, isn't he?"

Capezzi had consumed the last of the pizza. He washed it down with a long swig of diet Coke, of which he drank three two-liter bottles a day.

He put the bottle on the desk.

"We don't know. We know the guy who dropped the car off isn't."

"Cop?" The Ferret said it low, tentatively.

"Yeah. He's a cop."

The Ferret hoped his reaction played. Years of street survival informed his belly, and his belly told his head what to do.

"Fifty-third precinct. He's a Jew. Name is Howard Stein. Detective Third Grade."

"Jesus . . ."

Capezzi looked at him.

"I'm sorry, Mr. Capezzi," the Ferret said. "Very sorry."

"There is always the possibility your guy isn't."

The Ferret did not have to act disturbed. He was superdisturbed. There was a silence in the mobile home.

"How do you meet this guy?" Capezzi asked.

"Frank? I call him at home. Or I see him at Finnegan's."

"Would he be there now?"

"I don't know. If he's not there I can leave a message on his machine."

Tiny picked up a console phone on the desk and one of the gorillas grabbed it and set it in front of the Ferret.

"Call him now. Tell him you want to meet him in this Finnegan's. Tell him to bring his partner."

"For when?"

"Tomorrow, noon."

Shakily, the Ferret took out his address book and got Piccolo's number. Christ, they were going to whack two cops.

He punched it out. Thank God Tiny wasn't listening on the extension, even though they always played the role anyway. A mistake would be fatal.

The phone rang three times and then a recording came on.

"I got his answering machine," he said.

"Leave the message on the machine."

The Ferret left the message for Piccolo to meet him and then hung up.

"Should I call the bar?" the Ferret said.

Capezzi nodded.

The Ferret called. Piccolo wasn't there.

"That's okay," Tiny said. "But don't go home. I don't want him to be able to talk with you before tomorrow."

The Ferret nodded.

"Put on your clothes, August," Capezzi said. "You look like a plucked chicken."

He laughed, and the Ferret heard big rumbling laughter from one of the gorillas who flanked him and tittering laughter from the other.

Capezzi looked at one of the gorillas.

"Drive him to a motel here," Capezzi said. The Ferret watched Capezzi's eyes, which were trained on one of the gorillas. They were small, pig-like, dark, buried in folds of fat. It was hard to read them, hard to tell if they were saying something else.

Then the glint in them changed as he looked at the Ferret. "Okay," he said, "you fucked up. But you tried to help me, and I appreciate that. Next time be more careful."

"Thank you, Mr. Capezzi. I'm sorry "

"Get dressed."

As he dressed in silence the Ferret thought that he did not know if he was safe. He tended to think he was dead. All he could do was hope.

After he left, Capezzi thought that it was very bad

business for people to think undercover cops could get into his organization without being hurt.

Another object lesson was in order.

Frankenstein got home at around four in the morning.

The Ferret's message was the only one on the machine.

"Sounds a little nervous," Stein said.

"Yeah, I thought so. I wonder what's happening."

"We'll check it out in the morning."

CHAPTER 46

Within twelve hours, Lawless had something of a profile of Leo Molinari.

He was thirty-seven, a full-time actor, and had no yellow sheet.

Over the last two years, according to labor department records, he had been on unemployment three times and had lived in four different places, including Joplin, Missouri. The last known address they had on him was 221 East Ninth Street in the East Village.

Lawless and another felony squad cop named Art Hynes checked it out. It was a battered tenement very much like others in the area, a place probably run by one of those lizard landlords. On any given day you could go into a building like this and going door to door among users and drug dealers, make just about as many felony collars as you wanted.

Molinari was not there, and no one even remembered who he was except the super, an old bearded black guy who smelled like he bathed in Southern Comfort. He had seen Molinari once a month when he paid his rent.

But he hadn't seen him for four or five months.

"Around here," the super said, "you ain't got many tenants stay a long time."

Lawless then started what cops called "busywork," and he was aided in his efforts by Fred Billericks and two other guys from ATF. They started to check all the Molinaris listed in the phone books in all five boroughs. It was a door-to-door operation, time consuming and producing little results—except negative ones. It was the essence of police work.

There were three Leo Molinaris, two L. Molinaris, and one F. L. Molinari in the boroughs, and quite a few others without the first name or initial.

Through a phone company contact, Lawless also checked the unlisted Molinaris. There was one, an F. G. Molinari, and he or she lived in Staten Island.

The cops divided the work and paired off into two-man teams; the assumption was they were dealing with a headcase, and two men would be required if he was encountered.

They started to canvass.

CHAPTER 47

The day the detectives came to his mother's house, Bradley Fusari was inside it, upstairs in a bedroom. He did not attempt to get away because he was wise to the ways of the police. According to what his uncle had told his mother, they were coming over on a flyer; they couldn't possibly have time for a search warrant, and he had told his mother not to let them in.

He had stood at the top landing and listened to his mother talking to them. It thrilled him to be so close to prey; they were really the predators, but he had felt power over them.

Then, he had watched through a curtain upstairs as they walked down the driveway to their car.

The woman, he thought, was extraordinarily pretty and made something in his crotch crawl. She would be nice to fuck.

The man, who was big and paunchy, he figured to be about fifty-five. He looked like a typical tough bull. But bulls could be taken down, too.

After they drove away he got their cards from his mother, who wanted to know why they wanted to see him.

"You know how it is with ex-cons and cops, Ma," he said. " They harass us."

"You didn't do anything, right?"

"No. I've been good."

Inside, Fusari snickered. He knew his mother knew it was serious. It was just that she never wanted to believe anything bad about her little boy.

An hour after the detectives came, Bradley Fusari carefully checked around the house to make sure it wasn't being watched, then left out a back entrance, sneaking through a neighbor's yard to end up on a side street where he could walk away unobserved.

Luckily, his black Blazer was in the shop for a brake job. He would get that out, then take it to the city and put it in a garage. He assumed that if they were looking for *him* they would know his car and maybe put out an APB on it.

He had borrowed a hundred dollars from his mother before he left, though he actually didn't need it. He had gotten over five hundred dollars from the last couple he had taken down.

He just liked the idea of ripping her off.

He spent the night in a YMCA in the city, and the next morning was back on the island looking for a room.

146

He found one about ten o'clock in the morning in Smith-town.

The room was on the top floor of a two story colonial that had been converted into a series of rental units. The paint was faded and cracked and the ceiling had circular water marks on it. But it was cheap and off the beaten track, a good place to make a base of operations.

Once settled in, he taped the poster of Bruce Lee, the one where he is poised to strike, glowering dangerously at the camera, to the back of the closet door.

Bruce Lee had been his hero since he was six, and it was Bruce who had gotten him interested in karate.

Like Bruce, he was small and muscular and carried many more offensive weapons than one first realized.

Other cons found that out about him quickly in prison.

He was only there a few days when a big iron-pumping nigger who was to identify himself as Otis came up to him in the recreation yard and told him that from that moment on Otis was going to be his "friend," protect him from anyone who would try any "monkey stuff" with him.

At first, Fusari thought that was nice, but after a few minutes he got the idea and told Otis that he didn't want any part of it.

Otis said "I ain't giving you no choice on the deal. You my woman from now on."

Two days later, Otis approached him in the shower and told him to go into one of the toilet stalls with him, and Fusari had declined.

Then Otis had assaulted him, but Otis didn't understand something. From the time he had entered the shower and had seen Otis, Fusari had been descending into a state of akiru, meaning that at the very core of his being he was a placid, calm lake, while outside, in his limbs, he was the invincible fire. He would burn anyone who would try to violate him.

In front of a dozen other prisoners, Fusari took two minutes to disable Otis—who weighed almost twice what he did—to the point of hospitalization. And not the Attica infirmary: they didn't have the staff or equipment to fix all the broken bones and internal damage Fusari had done to Otis.

The prison grapevine is better than Western Union, and from that moment on Fusari was never bothered again by anyone. Predators treated him like a predator, which he knew he was. Indeed, after a couple of months he took his own "woman," a skinny blond kid who had started out prison life as a heterosexual.

One day soon after he took the room in Smithtown, Fusari started to feel the tension building, the sense of expanding inside, a slow, bubbling annoyance that gradually grew to anger, then rage.

He wanted to hurt someone.

He left the house on a Friday night at about five o'clock.

As he did, he started to feel better already. He was on the prowl, looking for prey.

Except he wasn't looking. He knew exactly where he was going.

He had stolen a car in Fort Lee, New Jersey, and equipped it with stolen Jersey plates from a car in another town.

As soon as he could, he would get New York State registration and inspection stickers for the car.

He took the Long Island Expressway into the city, and drove very carefully. He did not want to be stopped by a cop. If he was, he vowed that he would not be busted.

In the glove compartment, conceivably where he would reach for paperwork if stopped by a cop, was a 9 mm fourteen-shot automatic.

Twenty minutes later, the Throg's Neck Bridge to the Bronx came into view. He imagined himself as calm as a lake, but inside, swimming beneath the surface, was the powerful monster, waiting to emerge—and devour.

148

CHAPTER 48

After twelve hours of canvassing, Lawless and the ATF and squad guys had covered all of the Molinaris in the phone books.

A few weren't in, but of the ones they contacted none was the Molinari they were looking for.

The ATF guys went their way and the Five Three people went their's.

Lawless and Hynes went back to the squad room. Just before they got there, Lawless had an idea.

The labor department had Molinari as an actor, right?

Maybe he was in one of the professional organizations, like the Screen Actors Guild or AGVA.

Lawless called both.

Molinari was in AGVA.

To ease the job of getting the information, Lawless did some acting of his own.

"Yes," he said to the woman who answered, "my name is Dave Brown. I'm looking for Leo Molinari."

"Who are you?"

"I'm producer of the Spokane Repertory Theatre."

That stopped the woman. She couldn't be sure, Lawless thought, about what that was. And she probably didn't want to insult "Mr. Brown" by questioning him further.

Lawless laid it on thick.

"I understand from a friend of mine that Mr. Molinari is quite a good actor and would be perfect for a role I have. May I have his number?"

"We're not allowed to give them out."

"Really?" Lawless said, an edge in his voice. "How do actors get work?"

"I can give you the number of his agent."

"All right," Lawless said a trace pompously, "let me have that."

The woman went off the phone and came back a half minute later. Molinari's agent was someone named Irv Hoff. She gave Lawless the number.

Lawless did not thank her, but merely mumbled good-bye. Might as well play the rude theatrical role all the way.

He lit a cigarette before calling Irv Hoff. He was tense. If this was the perp, this could be it.

A man with a dulcet-toned voice answered the phone. He told Lawless, who identified himself as a producer, that Irv Hoff wasn't in.

"Where is he?" Lawless asked.

"In Europe."

Something clutched Lawless's innards.

"When will he be back?"

"A week."

"I see," Lawless said. "I was trying to get a hold of Leo Molinari. I think I have a role he'd be interested in."

"Oh. You know Leo's work?"

"A friend of mine saw him and thought he'd be good. What's his number?"

There was a little silence.

"I don't know if I'm allowed to give it."

Lawless chuckled.

"Well, if you don't he might regret it badly. I certainly can't wait until Mr. Hoff gets back to talk with Mr. Molinari."

Another smaller hesitation.

"His number is 718–555–8976."

"What's his address?"

Another hesitation. The man must have been wondering why Lawless would want his address. But he gave it.

"Twenty-three fourteen Vernon Avenue, Long Island City, 12867."

"Thank you very much."

"What was the name of the production company you're with?"

"Spokane Repertory."

"I see."

They hung up, and for the first time in weeks Lawless used the butt of the cigarette he was smoking to light another.

"Let's get a team together."

CHAPTER 49

Leo Molinari was in the kitchen of his home in Long Island City. He was sitting at the kitchen table sipping a cup of tea.

In every war, he thought, there are casualties.

Now, he knew, he was about to enter a phase of his own war where he could well be killed. He was entering his own personal D day. In a very real sense, it was as if he was in an LST, huddled, plowing through choppy waters under an overcast sky toward the beach at Normandy.

Today he could live, or he could die.

Curiously, he thought, I am not afraid.

But really it was not so curious. He knew there was a higher cause than his own life, a cause anointed by Jesus Chirst Our Lord. His life, in service to that cause, did not matter.

So, then, he was not concerned about his own death, except in one sense: one more soldier for Christ and the unborn would fall by the wayside.

His eyes teared.

His death did not matter. He would meet his Lord

and master in a better place than this, and there he would know life everlasting.

Outside, he heard a car door slam. He got up and went over to the window.

Sharon had just pulled her car into a parking space.

He was sorry about her.

The phone rang. He went over to the phone, which was mounted on the wall near the entrance to the kitchen, and picked up.

"Hello."

"Mr. Molinari?"

"Yes."

"Dale Howard from Mr. Hoff's."

"How are you, Dale?"

"Fine. Got some good news. A producer named Brown called and said that he had a gig for you."

"Where from?"

"Spokane Repertory Theatre."

"Never heard of it."

"Neither have I," Dale said. "I gave him your number, so he should be calling you."

"Good," Molinari said. "Did he mention the part?"

"No, but he said a friend of his had seen you on the boards and thought you'd be perfect for it—whatever it is."

"Thanks a lot, Dale."

They hung up.

Sharon came through the door carrying a package from the supermarket just as Molinari got the Spokane operator.

The operator tried to get the Spokane Repetory Theatre various ways, but without luck.

Sharon had taken off her coat and was putting the groceries away when Molinari got off the phone.

"What was that all about?" she said.

"Somebody may have another job for me."

"Good, Leo! Good! When it rains it pours."

Leo looked at her and smiled a funny little smile.

A moment later, he had gone out the door and was walking toward the shed.

CHAPTER 50

An hour after Sharon had returned from her shopping, Joe Lawless and Fred Billericks showed up. About the last thing the two cops wanted was a hostage-type situation, with Molinari inside and the cops outside, but they felt it necessary to have the house surrounded before they rang the bell, because the *very* last thing they wanted was for Molinari to escape.

There was no way to tell if Molinari was in. The streets had cars on them, but the DMV did not list him as the owner of a car. If one was his, they wouldn't know which one.

Lawless opened his suit jacket as he approached the door. The safeties on his holster and gun had been released.

He rang the bell and could hear it chiming inside. He heard movement inside, and tensed as the door opened.

It was a woman.

"Is Mr. Molinari here?"

She shook her head.

"No. Who are you?"

"Police officers," Lawless said. "May we come in?"

Her brow furrowed.

"What's the matter?"

"We can talk inside."

Inside, the woman, who identified herself as Sharon, explained that this was her house and that Leo Molinari was her fiancé. Had he done something wrong?

"No," Lawless said, "not necessarily. We just want to speak with him."

"He went out a half hour ago," she said.

"Is he coming back soon?" Billericks asked.

"I don't know, he doesn't tell me much."

"Do you mind," Lawless said, "if we look around?"

Sharon hesitated.

"I guess it's all right."

Lawless and Billericks walked through the rooms.

They were typically middle-class, except perhaps for the religious artifacts. Molinari or the woman or both were obviously religious. Which fit. Lawless remembered what Billericks told him about the bomber couples in the south: they were very religious.

There was nothing specifically, though, to suggest to either cop that Molinari, or the woman, was a bomber.

Of course they could not turn the place over as they normally would because they didn't have a warrant, and the woman could tell them to get the hell out anytime she wished.

They were in the bedroom—the woman had stayed in the living room—and Lawless was on his way out the door when Billericks whispered to him. He was standing by a chest of drawers, seemingly mesmerized by something in a drawer he had opened.

Lawless came over and looked and felt his heart rate leap.

Lying on a white towel was a bottle, and inside was the twenty-week-old fetus.

Suspicion had turned to certainty.

Lawless and Billericks left the house without telling the woman what they had found.

"Thanks for your help. Just tell him to call us when he comes in, okay?" Lawless said, handing the woman his card.

"Everything okay?"

"Yes."

They pulled the team off Molinari's house, then drove a few blocks away, where they regrouped.

They decided to put three two-man surveillance teams on the house. It was going to be tough duty because it was cold out, and sitting motionless in a car that can only occasionally be fired up is not the way to stay warm.

Lawless ordered two surveillance vans by radio, but these would take a little while to put in place.

Once the surveillance was in place, all the cops could do was hope that Molinari would come back.

Molinari wasn't coming back.

Ten minutes after Lawless and Billericks left the house he called, and his voice sounded strange. Indeed, he had acted kind of strange when he had said good-bye to Sharon. He seemed happy and sad at the same time, and he kissed her deeply, with more feeling than he had ever displayed before.

It had worried Sharon, and made her happy at the same time.

The purpose of his call became clear.

He wanted to know if they had had any visitors.

"Yes, the police were here," she said, and then explained what had happened.

"What do they want, Leo?"

"Old business," he said, and she heard a lilt of laughter in his voice. "As old as time. Good-bye."

And then he was gone, and Sharon was staring at the phone, knowing something bad was going to happen. She started to cry.

CHAPTER 51

Barbara's business card had led Fusari to her.

He had followed her for three days before finding out that she lived in an apartment off Pelham Bay Avenue in the Bronx. He had been particularly careful with her because she was a cop; she wasn't the average person who would not notice anything.

Fusari had no idea whether she lived with someone or not. So far, when she came home from the station, she came home alone.

During the day, when she was not there, he had checked the mailboxes: there was no Babalino listed.

He had also gone to her apartment door on the first floor. The door was metal, heavily braced and with a couple of locks, probably deadbolts. Fusari didn't expect anything less from a cop. They knew that there were bad guys out there.

He also had listened by her door, but had not been able to hear any sound coming from inside.

He would have to be very careful, he knew, about where he would take her down, and when. Surprise had to be everything. She certainly had a gun and knew how to use it. She was a good-looking gash, but she wasn't in this precinct because she was a pussy.

Fusari knew that she would recognize him, even if he wore a mask.

But he had no intention of wearing a mask. He wouldn't need one. When he had used her he would kill her. She wouldn't identify anyone.

Fusari knew that he was ripe to kill. He had been building toward it a long time.

This was the perfect time. He would kill her, then he would go out to Suffolk and kill the fuzz. But first he would turn him into a punk.

These were thoughts that Fusari could not have without getting aroused almost to the point of ejaculation.

CHAPTER 52

Frankenstein decided that it didn't even pay to go to bed. When they had returned from Philadelphia it was four in the morning. They were to meet the Ferret at noon, and they were also going to drop a dime to Stein's guy in Chester, Pa. first thing. Piccolo also wanted to call his nephew Danny, who had started the whole thing going. He wanted to tell him that he thought he had a shot at getting his rig back, that he saw many Peterbilts in the warehouse—maybe one was his.

So, instead of going to bed, they broke out a bottle of cold guinea red.

They sat in the kitchen and sipped it, and this time Piccolo had the same kind of feeling that he had when Eddie was alive. Fantastic. Him and his buddy sipping wine, quiet all around except for the gentle stirring of the python in its cage. The good times were definitely here again.

Piccolo looked across the table at Howie.

"Hey my man, how you doin'?"

"Very well indeed," Stein said, "very well indeed."

And they lifted their glasses in a toast.

"To Frankenstein," Stein said.

"To Frankenstein," Piccolo said, and they quaffed their drinks.

He raised this to me back She looked at it. An
she saw it.
A reached for the phone

CHAPTER 53

Sharon sat on the edge of her bed. She slowly twisted her hands.

It had now been an hour since Leo called. She knew Leo was going to blow up some place. People could die. He could die.

Unless . . . unless she stopped him.

God, she thought, he would be so mad at her if she tried to do that. He would probably never talk to her again.

The idea of Leo not talking to her made her feel hollow and empty, and brought her close to tears.

She loved Leo so. Leo was such a good person, really. A caring person. It was just this one bad thing he had about abortion.

If only he didn't have that.

She twisted her hands more tightly together.

What would she do if he died? How would she live? How would she survive on the earth without Leo? Her life would have no meaning for her

But he would leave here, too, if she contacted the police and tried to stop him.

Tears came to her eyes. She didn't know what to do.

She stood up and started to pace back and forth across the bedroom.

Maybe nothing would happen. Maybe everything would be all right. Maybe she was worrying too much.

She stopped pacing. She didn't believe it.

He had just sounded too strange on the phone.

She went out of the bedroom and into the kitchen.

The card the detective had given her was on the table.

She picked it up, looked at it. An immense sadness suffused her.

She turned and reached for the phone.

CHAPTER 54

For well over two hours after he left the house, Leo Molinari wandered around the city, wondering what to do.

It was not just enough, he decided, to blow up the J & L butcher shop, or Bronx General—which he had also considered. But it was important to make a statement. Without a clear message, everything he had done would be for nought.

But he did not know how to do that, so, in the end, he turned to Jesus, going once again to the holy place in Fresh Meadows. He knelt and prayed to God for guidance, and, finally, guidance came.

He knew then what he had to do.

A half hour later, Leo got off the subway at Tremont Avenue and started to walk north toward the J & L Clinic.

It was a fairly warm day—in a couple of weeks it would be spring—and there were some people on the street, but he could not see anyone guarding the butcher shop.

Not that that meant someone wasn't watching. Or that there wasn't a heavy guard inside.

In his mind, there was no question that they were on to him.

What they didn't know was that he didn't care. All he cared about was the statement. To make that as clear as he could, to let it be heard around the world.

Up the block, parked on the street a few cars up from the J & L Clinic, in a tan car, were Joe Lawless and Art Hynes.

Art was covering the east side of Tremont and Lawless the west. There was no way that Molinari could approach J & L without being seen.

And it was not only J & L that was covered; all of the other clinics in the Bronx were under surveillance and on the alert. In fact, Lawless had urged the clinics to shut down for the rest of the day. Two had agreed, but the rest, including J & L, had not.

The extraordinary measures had been triggered by a call from Molinari's girlfriend, Sharon: she was afraid that today Leo was going to do something bad. She didn't know what, but she just felt it coming.

She begged Lawless not to hurt Leo, and Lawless said he would do everything in his power to accomplish that, if Leo did show up.

As he scanned the area, Lawless at first didn't spot Molinari ambling up the block toward the J & L Clinic. The original perp had dark hair and a moustache and glasses, and for a moment that image was in Lawless's brain. Molinari was now sans disguise, and he had long blond hair that for a moment was a detail that didn't trigger a response.

But then it did, and Lawless could see the FD photo, the dark, demented eyes staring out from beneath the shock of blond hair.

"Art," he said, low and urgent, "He's coming toward us, north."

As nonchalantly as possible, they got out of the car and engaged in an animated conversation as they approached Molinari. The idea was to grab him as he went by.

They were ten yards from Molinari, who was another ten yards from the entrance to J & L, when it happened.

Suddenly, Molinari opened the long coat he was wearing. The sight was stunning.

His chest was covered with tied-together sticks of dynamite. One hand was free, but the other was still in a pocket.

"I figured you were cops," he said, extremely calmly. "Let me tell you something. You're looking at an open-circuit alarm system attached to forty sticks of dynamite. If my hand relaxes because you have a sharpshooter shoot me in the head we go boom. Back off!"

There was absolutely nothing they could do. They backed off, and Molinari entered the J & L Clinic.

A minute later, to their surprise, J & L personnel started pouring out of the clinic.

One of them rushed up to Lawless, who had pinned his shield to his jacket while Hynes rushed to the car to call for backup.

She was a young Hispanic nurse.

"He said clear the area and call the media. He'll give you twenty minutes."

Just then a blue and white, bubble gum lights on, pulled up. Lawless barked a command.

"Get people off the block and out of the buildings in a two block area. There's a bomber inside."

Twenty minutes later, Leo Molinari emerged from the J & L Clinic, which had been emptied of everyone, including a woman who had been anesthetized and was about to have an abortion performed.

As he appeared, people involuntarily stepped back even further, though no one was within seventy yards of him, and they were all cops dressed in flak jackets and helmets. The media were behind the cops.

Molinari spoke, his voice projecting through the empty street as if it were a canyon. His arms were stretched outward; his voice thrummed with feeling.

"Today, I make a statement, a protest against those who would still the lives of the yet-unborn children who have every right to walk on God's earth.

"Today, as I join my savior in Heaven, I go with the full knowledge that while I lived on this earth I delivered a message that will never be forgotten.

"I could have taken many lives with me, but that is not God's way. God is not cruel, God is not murderous, God is merciful and just. Only one life will go today—mine. I will gladly and proudly join my Jesus. I will be impaled on my own cross next to my savior.

"So I say this to all my colleagues across this land: do not weep for me. I join my Heavenly Father, and let my death always be remembered as a statement that little ones yet unborn may live. Never give up the fight.

"Good-bye my darling Sharon, I will always love you."

One of the cops screamed, "Wait."

But it was too late. Molinari waved good-bye and went back into the clinic.

Involuntarily, cops started to back off even more.

A moment later, a good piece of Tremont Avenue was gone.

And so, very apparently, was Leo Molinari.

CHAPTER 55

Barbara Babalino parked her car in front of the building where she lived, set her alarm, and exited the car, making sure the doors were locked behind her.

"I don't see him," she said, apparently to thin air. But it wasn't thin air. She was wired, and a backup team of cops—including Bickford on special assignment—was listening. Three of the cops were in a van a less than fifty yards away, and two were in an empty apartment on the second floor in the same building where Barbara had her apartment.

162

She was frustrated.

For three nights she knew Fusari was following her, then he was gone. Maybe one of the backup teams had taken a burn without realizing it. If so, they were going to have to arrest Fusari and try to convict him on what they had.

But they didn't have much—particularly since he had worn gloves and a mask.

Barbara entered her building.

She half expected an attack from Fusari in the foyer of her building, but there was nothing.

Then again, at her door, she half expected him to emerge and try to push her inside.

But he didn't.

She entered, then relocked the door behind her. There was no way he could get in the door, and though she lived on the first floor and the windows were accessible, they were covered with bars.

Barbara checked all the rooms. Empty. She was dis appointed.

"He's not inside, he's not outside. Mr. Wrigley's isn't showing tonight. Good night folks."

Barbara undressed, took the wire off, then took a shower.

She was aware, as she did, that Joe and she could be spending a little time together from now on. The bomber case had ended—tragically, but it was fortunate that no one else died except the bomber.

And one way or another she was going to have to wrap the Wrigley's case up soon.

She decided to hit the hay right away, and as she went into the bedroom she smelled again the sharp, pleasant smell she had noticed when she had first checked the room.

Perhaps, she thought, Joe had changed after-shaves.

She put out the light and climbed into bed, plunging the room into blackness.

Barbara had been in bed for less than a minute when suddenly, chillingly, she sensed that she was not alone in the room. Someone was there with her.

Then she remembered something one of the victims, Ketcham, had said.

The rapist wore Polo after-shave.

God.

How did he get in?

For a moment, she felt panic starting to envelop her, but then she remembered something. Once before she had been alone in the room with a psychopath, and she was still alive.

But she had a major problem: her gun was in the living room. And there were no weapons in the room.

She didn't have any weapon, then, either, but she had survived.

But Fusari—it had to be Fusari—was a karate expert. She could only handle him with a gun.

Where was he?

There was only one place. Her closet was too narrow to hide him, and she had stuff hung in it—he wasn't there.

Her mind screeched. He was under the bed.

Her mind worked like a trip-hammer. He would make an attack at any moment.

What was she going to do? What . . . ?

Could she make it out of the bed to her gun in the living room?

Could she make it to the front door?

Even if she did, there were so many locks on it. . . .

Scream . . . to whom? Maybe Baines and Virag, the cops in the second floor apartment, were still there.

No, they were long gone.

Oh God, she wished Joe were here.

An idea: she realized she would only get one chance.

She coughed, then said out loud, "Dammit. Should have remembered that."

And then she put the light on and, feeling as if at any moment he would grab her ankles, she made her way over to her dresser.

It was there. A can of hair spray.

She took a deep breath and turned. The bed covers went almost to the floor, but she could see the slightest movement below them.

"Okay shithead," she said, "come out with your hands up!"

For a moment there was nothing, and then there was movement—two hands appeared on the side of the bed and Fusari pulled himself out.

It all happened in a millisecond.

He could see that Barbara had no gun, just a can of hair spray in her hand, and he started to move. She put the can within six inches of his eyes and squeezed.

He screamed in agony.

Then Barbara was through the door and into the living room. Behind her she heard him coming out of the bedroom. She ripped her .38 from the holster, and then turned and went into a modified Weaver stance.

Fusari was framed in the door.

"Freeze or die, you fuck!"

In his hand was a 9 mm automatic, and Barbara waited.

Fusari froze, and Barbara could tell that he could hardly see.

"On your belly," she growled. "You've brought a lot of pain to a lot of people. I'd have no problem shooting you."

Fusari dropped the gun and got on his belly.

CHAPTER 56

In the morning, Frankenstein called the Ferret at his home, but he wasn't there.

Piccolo also called Finnegan's. He didn't expect to find him there, but he just wanted to call anyway. Jake, the owner, said he wasn't there—and he hadn't seen him the night before.

That, Piccolo thought, was unusual. The Ferret was usually at Finnegan's every night.

In discussion, it was decided that Stein would not call his contact at the Chester police until they had spoken with the Ferret, so he could stay away from the warehouse when the cops descended on it.

They were getting ready to leave the house for their meeting at Finnegan's when Stein, who was putting on his jacket, said, "What's the matter Frank? Is something wrong?"

Piccolo, who had not yet dressed, smiled and nodded.

"I guess there is, but I don't know what. I just don't know."

"I'm not understanding you, Frank."

Piccolo smiled again.

"I don't fucking understand myself. It's just . . . I don't know if we should go to this meeting."

"Why not?"

"I don't know. I can't put my finger on anything. I just smell danger."

Stein nodded.

"Frank," he said, "let me say something. I think that you went though a terrible thing with Eddie, and it's still got you a little spooked. Maybe you think you're going to lose me, too."

Piccolo nodded.

"Maybe you're right," he said, "but Capezzi has a reputation for whacking undercovers. I just don't know. My fucking antenna is up."

There was a silence for a moment.

"Okay, let's go," Piccolo said, "but do me one favor. Let's wear some body armor."

"Really?"

"It'll help keep you warm," Piccolo said, and smiled. But inside he was not smiling.

At ten to twelve, Frankenstein approached Finnegan's.

Stein was relaxed, but Piccolo was not. He had spent years on the streets of Siberia, developing his already sharp street radar into a sensitive instrument. On the street, many times, all you had to go on was your instinct. Later, you might be able to figure out logically why you felt the way you did, but that was later.

It was instinct now, and Piccolo was alert to danger from everywhere. On the street . . . in the bar . . . on the rooftops . . . any fucking thing, where you least expected it.

The danger came, and when it did Piccolo saw it coming, all the way up 161st Street. It was a car, with Pennsylvania plates, and Piccolo knew right away that there were shooters in it.

The car was parked, and Piccolo made a quick decision. "Howie, shooters in a car. Go down."

Stein went down just a millisecond before the car started to roar toward them. Two shooters were hanging out the side windows with heavy artillery.

From under his coat, Piccolo took out the alley gun, which would yield excellent results for anyone adroit enough to squeeze the trigger.

He pointed the gun and squeezed the trigger, and as he did yelled, "Come on, motherfuckers! Come on!"

But they couldn't. The gunfire shattered all the windows, and within four seconds the driver and the two shooters were dead, and then, just like in the movies, the car careened slowly out of control and was on its side, wheels spinning at sixty miles an hour.

Piccolo, followed by Stein, ran up to it.

"Hey," Piccolo yelled, his eyes glinting wildly. "Where the fuck is the fucking fire? It's very unsatisfying without a fucking fire."

And then Piccolo and Stein were laughing in chorus, with a laugh that would have done Dr. Frankenstein proud.

EPILOGUE

Barbara found out how Fusari got into the apartment the day they arrested him: through the dumbwaiter. He had gone into the basement with a short ladder, leaned it up inside the shaft, climbed up and then had pried open the dumbwaiter door to gain access. He had pulled the ladder up inside the apartment and put it under the bed with him until Barbara had come home.

He said he planned to attack her when she entered the apartment, but didn't because he was hiding in the bedroom when she came in and had overheard her speaking into the wire.

Unfortunately, his victims—except for Joan Keenan—had to be told about Fusari being HIV positive.

All were tested, but none showed the AIDS virus. They could only pray that they didn't have the disease.

Onairuts, the medical examiner, told Lawless that there was exactly twelve pounds, four ounces of Leo Molinari left to bury. At least that is what they could recover.

His story—his message—stayed on the front pages for exactly one day, and then was gone.

A memorial service was held for him, and it was well attended by right-to-life groups.

Sharon was told by Lawless that she was not responsible for Molinari's death, but she had a hard time accepting that. Her Leo was gone forever, and even if she did survive—and she was not sure she would—there would always be a great empty space inside her for him. She knew, too, that every time she saw a baby she would think of Leo.

It was all so terribly sad. . . .

Frankenstein kept it simple. Stein called Spagnoli, his contact in the Chester police, and told him about the warehouse, but had him treat the call as an anonymous tip.

As it happened, the cops made their raid on the warehouse exactly ten hours before the cars and eighteen wheelers were set to be shipped to South America.

They collared about twenty-five people. Whether or not they could flip one or more so they could take down Capezzi was debatable.

And Danny Parilli, Piccolo's nephew, got his Peterbilt back.

The whole deal, Frankenstein figured, hurt Capezzi bad.

But as they sat in the apartment drinking wine, there was nothing to celebrate, aside from the fact that they had not been whacked.

The Ferret was nowhere to be found, and Frankenstein knew, sadly, that he was history.

Piccolo stared at the table.

"He was a good guy," Piccolo said. "He would have made a good cop. It's fucking sad."

"Yeah, that fat hump just whacks people—cops, anybody. He's got balls."

"You're right, Howie," Piccolo said. "But we're gonna make 'em hurt. First chance we get we're going to Philly and give him something to remember the Ferret by—and take his balls back to the Bronx."

Stein raised his glass and Frankenstein drank.

"That's a promise," Stein said.

About the Author

Tom Philbin is the son and grandson of cops. His previous *Precinct: Siberia* novels are PRECINCT: SIBERIA, UNDER COVER, COP KILLER, A MATTER OF DEGREE, JAMAICA KILL and STREET KILLER. He lives on Long Island.

PRECINCT: SIBERIA...

the 53rd precinct is a burned-out landscape where hookers
and pimps, junkies and killers, outnumber law-abiding
citizens. It's where they exile the cops who are
too violent, too corrupt, or too independent
to make it downtown.

by
Tom Philbin
from
Fawcett Books